Tripping

Abby Williams.

Abby Williams

Tripping

First Edition

This edition published in 2016
BY EXCALIBUR PRESS

ISBN: 978-0-9935015-4-8

Formatting & layout by
EXCALIBUR PRESS

EXCALIBUR PRESS
Belfast, Northern Ireland

excaliburbelfast@gmail.com
07982628911 | @ExcaliburPress
www.excaliburpress.co.uk

DEDICATION

Thank you to all the people I've met and the crazy experiences we've had together over the last eight years.
You all helped to create Tripping.
Mostly, thank you to my ever supportive family and friends for putting up with me.
I appreciate and love you more than you know.

Chapter 1

I opened Pandora's Box, and no one warned me. All I know is I'm hollow, as if someone has scraped out my insides with a rusty spoon. And tired, so tired. He's gone. They're all gone. And I can't see past this thick black fog ahead. I don't even know if there's a way back, but I want to forget. I want it all erased from memory. Three months, that's all it took. I'm all used up, and nothing's how it was.

The thin needle penetrates my vein, a crimson stream trickling into the clear tube like a tiny red snake. I watch it for a moment, my head resting heavily on the thin pillow that smells of cheap detergent.

'The doctor will need a urine sample, too.'

The student nurse is young, probably my age. She's wearing far too much eyeliner. 'Scarlet.' she says firmly.

She sounds like my Mum, sighing before placing a plastic container on my bedside locker. When she's gone I roll over onto my side and close my eyes. All I can smell are those harsh chemicals. Most people hate that smell, but I don't mind. It reminds me of cocaine, and all the mysterious rubbish it's usually mixed with that is probably more harmful than the drug itself. A nice, potent key of it now would alleviate so much of this heaviness.

I remember taking my first line. I was 18, and it was the summer after I left school. The immediate rush of confidence it induced was like a splash of icy cold water first thing in the morning. I loved how it injected colour into everything, how it showed you the world in HD. I just wanted everything to be beautiful, all the time. All anyone really wants is to feel good, and illicit substances are a shortcut past all the daily bullshit we have to put up within our lives. It's cheating, of course. But no one ever gave me a rule book on how to live my life, so I made up my own.

'Look at that beauty.' Deano breathed, racking up a thin line of coke with the speed and precision of only a seasoned user.

'Don't be stingy, give me a proper one.' I said half-jokingly, eyes fixed on the glass table that had served as part of our narcotic apparatus from the moment we moved in last summer.

'When have you ever known me to be stingy?' Deano's eyes flickered in anticipation. Despite his chronic moodiness, even he still felt the thrill of opening a brand new bag of charlie.

'Here, space cadet. Want some?' Lauryn broke her daydream and looked at me as if she had just come out of a coma.

'What do you think?' She flashed a grin and lazily ruffled her mop of white-blonde hair . She had opted for a pixie cut a few months ago, but now it had grown she was constantly twiddling the little strands between her delicate fingers. Nothing seemed to phase her, I realised with a hint of envy.

I watched Lauryn sniff her line, coughing and giggling at the same time as the coke smacked her full swing in the face. We had managed to obtain the good stuff, the kind that jiggles your insides instantly and makes you shudder with pleasure. She passed me the fiver and sat back, sighing contentedly. Hungrily, I hunched over the table and pressed my nose to the note, inhaling deeply. I felt the bitter white powder shoot up my left nostril, before it fused with saliva and steadily dripped down the back of my throat. I smiled and grimaced in sync. That foul, beautiful taste tells me in a matter of seconds I will be where I want to be...High. Why would I ever want to come down? Cocaine was the answer to so many questions, and it turned us into demi-gods. The kind of person you think is really awesome but you never thought you could be. Well, the good gear does anyway, the crap stuff is nothing more than a placebo. But if it does the job, then who really cares? The only problem was staying high.

Being twenty-something in Belfast meant we were never far from our next hit. It was 2014, the place was riddled with the stuff. Users were getting younger and prices were rising. The city was in an intermediate period of growth, far enough past the Troubles to be of growing interest to foreigners, but not far enough to lose the stagnant religious tensions between a remaining few who held on to the past with endless perseverance. Deano preached that it was only a matter of time before life as we knew it would cease to exist, that we were going backwards instead of forwards. I wasn't entirely sure what he meant but I figured it was all the more reason to seize the day.

'Here's to freedom.' Deano said from beneath the soft brown curls of his almost-beard, wiping the snowy remnants off the glass and rubbing them enthusiastically on his gums.

'Or failure.' I raised an eyebrow, 'I'm the smart one remember?'

'I think you'll find that's me,' he snorted. I couldn't really argue with someone who read books as thick as loaves of bread about Quantum Physics for pleasure. 'But you're right,' he continued, momentary obnoxiousness aside, 'you are smart. Which is why nursing was never going to be enough for you.'

'There are some very intelligent nurses.' I protested, lighting a cigarette.

'Probably. But it's not who you are. You'd have always wanted more.'

I sighed in agreement, carelessly flicking ash into one of the several beer cans that littered the floor, remnants of the weekend's drunken shenanigans.

Early the day before I had climbed about six flights of stairs to the Head of Nursing, Mr. Nolan's, office and hesitated before my hand reached up to knock on the door.

'Come in.' a voice bellowed.

I shuffled into the small office, drenched in sickly yellow light, and closed the door behind me. Books, folders and files of every description were piled high on shelves that stretched from floor to ceiling. Mr. Nolan was writing enthusiastically at his desk, cluttered with several empty coffee cups and mountains of paper. He didn't look up. I cleared my throat.

'I hope you're not busy...'

He scribbled something on a post-it note and stuck it on one of the desk drawers. Then he exhaled, took off his glasses and began wiping the lenses with his tie.

'I'm always busy. What can I help you with?'

He returned his glasses to the bridge of his broad nose and peered up at me before motioning for me to sit down.

'Thanks.'

I hurriedly took a seat opposite him and tried to keep my eyes from straying to the huge, shiny bald patch on the top of his head. It was as if he'd been polishing it. He looked down again and began scanning his notes.

'Well?' He tapped his pen on the edge of the desk.

'Sorry,' I mumbled, fumbling with the strap of my bag. Best to just come out with it, I thought. 'It's just, well, I want to leave the course.'

The pen-tapping stopped abruptly and he looked up at me curiously.

'And why would that be?' He raised a hair, grey eyebrow.

Unexpectedly, he didn't sound too surprised. I assumed he's try and talk me out of it, give me the old speech about wasting opportunities and 'my future'.

'I just...I made a mistake. I don't think nursing is for me.' I explained.

He was silent, just chewing the top of his pen and observing me thoughtfully over the top of those thick glasses.

'What do you propose to do instead?' he asked eventually.

Christ, it was like I was on trial.

'That's the thing. I'm not sure. All I know is I rushed into it because I thought it was the right thing to do and I need a break to figure it all out.'

I failed to mention that the course bored me senseless and I felt like I was slowly suffocating. And the fact that all this coursework was massively interfering with my drug-taking.

'And you're certain that's what you want?'

'Yes, sir. Yes it is,' I paused. 'You see, I've already left...in my head. I'd rather not waste any more of my time, or yours.'

He peered at me intently until I became a little uncomfortable.

'Then you must leave in body,' he said eventually, straightening his back. 'I won't try and convince you otherwise, if that's what you've decided.'

'It is.' I said, relieved that I had avoided a big lecture.

I made to leave.

'What does concern me,' he began, and I froze in my seat, 'is how things will unfold for you henceforth.'

Great, I spoke to soon. Who even says 'henceforth'? It's not even a real word anymore. I looked at him, confused.

'I'm not sure what you mean.'

Please don't start banging on about me 'wasting my skills' or 'letting myself down', I pleaded internally.

'Some form of structure, a focus, is healthy. It gives us balance. You're a bright girl, capable of doing anything you set your mind to. I see a lot of potential in you, a great thirst for life. But with that comes the potential for it to be channeled in the wrong ways, in damaging ways.'

I had no idea what he was blathering on about, to be honest. I just wanted to get out of there.

'Well, thank you for being understanding.'

I stood up and he reached out to shake my hand.

'Just keep your head.' Mr. Nolan said.

I smiled in an effort to show appreciation before diving towards the door. I heard him shout 'Good luck!' after me, which pissed me off a bit. I didn't need his luck.

Now here I was. No responsibilities, nothing to tie me down, and all three of us were restless. It had been just over a year since Lauryn and I had been thrust into that twilight zone between adolescence and full maturity, armed with very little but our grade certificates and copious amounts of cheap beer. Lauryn had survived the transition with me while others fell by the wayside. The three of us had spent the past year working, studying or both, and had found that cocaine interposed a wonderful dose of excitement in our otherwise mundane lives. It was the perfect distraction when the massive array of life choices made me want to drop out of the mainstream altogether.

'Maybe I should have taken a year out after school.' I pondered aloud, 'Gone to help orphans in Africa or something.'

'You can help orphans here, you don't have to go to Africa.' Deano said.

'I just don't want to be tied down, to anything.' I moaned.

'Stop your whinging.'

'At least you got rid of Luke.' Lauryn said with her usual

optimism.

'The old ball and chain.' Deano grunted.

'Deano, we were together for four months. It was hardly a marriage.'

'You may as well have been married, he made you miserable.'

'Well, not anymore. He's long gone.' I said.

'Sweet, you can stay out past your bed time now.' Deano said with a smirk.

'Hilarious.' I nodded towards the table, 'Do us out another, please?'

'I have to go to work in like, twenty-one hours.' Lauryn sighed, glancing at her watch.

I sat up and ran my finger along the glass table to collect the left over powder and tasted the sour crumbs on my tongue.

'How do you survive an eight hour shift cleaning old lady bums without taking coke with you?'

She shrugged. 'I don't usually need it. Plus I don't want to get caught. Can you imagine how embarrassing that would be? All the nice old ladies thinking I'm a druggie or something.'

'You're not a druggie unless you're living in a squat and selling your shoes for a line.' I assured her.

'This place is starting to look like a squat.' Deano looked around at the mess and shook his head before pushing the DVD case towards me.

'We're recreational users. Not the same thing.' I snorted the line in one swift movement. 'As long as you've got control of it then there's no harm done'

'Is this the type of thing people say to each other to rationalise their drug-taking?' Deano said.

'Probably.'

The three of us let out a snort of laughter. People were always trying to make things out to be something their not, especially when it came to drugs. Everyone loved an opportunity to offload their judgment and make themselves feel like superior humans. But it was just the way things were for us, it's not like I couldn't stop if I really wanted to. I imagined life without gear would be a series of greys, nothing like the colourful peaks and troughs of our turbulent but thrilling coke-fueled reality. That's all I needed to know. For the moment, anyway.

Lauryn had wriggled round onto her stomach, reached for her bag and fumbled around in it until she found her video camera. Flipping it open, she turned to me.

'Smile.' She ordered, those big green eyes focusing intently on the little screen.

She always had that thing with her, ever since she'd taken a weekend course in filmography. I vaguely recall her explaining to me the importance of capturing things in the moment, because everything got lost and misconstrued in hindsight. I did begin to question this once I walked in on her recording a daddy longlegs flinging itself around a windowsill. As much as I was a patron of the arts, documenting the lives of ugly insects did not appeal to me. I pulled a face before scanning round the room for another cigarette.

'Tell us how you feel about your newfound freedom,' she giggled.

'If you can call it that,' I mumbled, locating the packet of Mayfair and extracting another cigarette with my lips. I laid back flat on the floor, lit my cigarette and inhaled deeply, 'I'm going to dedicate the next three months to complete freedom. From jobs, or uni or any of that crap.'

Deano sniggered and I glared at him.

'What? You think I can't do it?'

'No, I'm more afraid that you *will* do it.' he said.

'Well, I will. I'm sick of being pressured into making decisions. When do we actually get the time to sit back and think for ourselves?' I threw the cigarette in the ash tray and flopped my arms down by my sides.

'I think that's the idea.' Deano muttered, forever the anti-establishment anarchist that he was at heart. He'd been the same way ever since we met a year ago, at one of those awkward Freshers Fayre meetings for the Book Club. With rather wealthy parents who had expected him to conform to the family line of dentists, Deano had used their financial platform to do quite the opposite: study Physics and rely comfortably on their monthly allowance. He was an open-minded realist, some might say. To me, he was someone who had his head screwed on, substance abuse issues aside.

'And I'll make a bucket list.' I announced.

'You're not dying.' Deano objected.

'So?'

'So...you have a bucket list to complete before you die, not for the summer.'

'I can if I want!'

'Fine.'

'What's on your list?' Lauryn asked curiously.

'Well, now I'm single, I want to have really great sex.'

'Any sex would be good...' Deano grumbled.

'And I want to trip on acid.' I continued.

'I'm in on that.' He perked up instantly.

I toyed with my lighter thoughtfully for a moment.

'Oh, and I want to party for five straight days and nights.'

'Your bucket list will come in handy in that case. You might just die.' Deano said.

'No one's going to *die*, granddad. It's a social experiment.'

'A social experiment?' he scoffed, 'To see how fucked you can get over the next three months?'

'Don't act like you aren't going to join in.'

'I want to meet more people. Exciting people.' Lauryn interjected.

'And spend more time in nature.' I added.

'We were at the park last week.' Deano said.

'That's not exactly nature.'

'Okay, okay.'

'It's going to be the best summer of our lives, I promise,' I said excitedly, 'Ninety days of totally uncensored, unforgettable madness! Are you in?'

'I'm in!' Lauryn high-fived me and we both looked expectantly at Deano. He puffed hard on his cigarette and rolled his eyes.

'Oh, Okay. I guess if everyone else is,' he sighed. Then he looked at us and a grin spread across his face, 'I couldn't exactly let you two loose by yourselves.'

I clapped my hands with glee.

'Another bump to celebrate?'

I didn't even need to ask. Deano poured out a generous pile and made us each a thick line. Suddenly, Lauryn took a sharp intake of breath and sat bolt upright.

'What's wrong?' Deano eyes her warily.

'My video camera.' she waved it above her head.

'What about it?' I asked.

'I'll video our whole summer on it. I can edit it and make it into a short film for us to keep.'

Tripping

'This is the best idea!' I squealed, knocking over the ashtray and dusting the carpet with fresh fag ash.

'To be fair, all of our ideas seem great when we're high.' Deano looked at me skeptically and then laughed.

'Let's do it,' Lauryn pointed the video camera directly at me.

I shielded my face against the sudden exposure with my hand.

'We'll start now.' I said.

'Now?' Lauryn's eyes were as wide a saucers.

'No time like the present. What time will Enya be here?'

Enya was one of those 'hippy freaks', according to Luke. The type that used 'bad' drugs like pills and trips. I guess it was both fear and his possessiveness that had stopped me dabbling in anything aside from coke. But the allure was always there...what better time to see what all the fuss was about?

At that moment my phone beeped.

'Is it him?' Lauryn asked as I reached over and grabbed it from my bag. I checked the screen and sighed.

'No, it's Mum. Checking I'm still alive. I haven't called her in over a week.'

'Have you told her about leaving your course?' Lauryn asked.

'Nope.'

She looked at me, concerned.

'At least it wasn't Luke checking up on you again.' Deano pointed out.

'I've deleted his number anyway.'

I chucked my phone into my bag.

'The final step out of the door to independence.' He mused, probably pleased that he wouldn't have to hear me whine about how frustrating Luke was anymore.

'Something like that So, we're going to do this?'

'Definitely,' Lauryn nodded enthusiastically.

Deano shook his head at us with a smile. 'Enya just text, she's on her way.'

'Brilliant, get her to bring a bottle of vodka.' I sat up and peered around the room for empty glasses.

'So it begins.' Deano sighed, puffing his cigarette down to the butt before stubbing it out in the ashtray.

Chapter 2

Enya smiled at us with lips the shade of warm cherry as she floated into the living room, her auburn dreadlocks dangling just below her shoulders like little pieces of furry rope. She collapsed onto the sofa beside Lauryn, a plastic bag containing various bottles clanking as they hit the floor.

'How long have you lot been on it?' She asked before extracting a pouch of tobacco from her coat.

'A while.' I smiled.

'Nutters.' She laughed and started rolling a joint. 'Where's the tunes?'

Enya peered around until she located the speakers and turned up the volume until vigorous drum and bass filled the corners of the room. As the music flowed, our senses were stimulated once more and a new influx of energy began to gather speed.

Not only did I have the freedom to properly celebrate the luxury of being idle, the mere presence of Deano and Enya meant that a catalogue of drugs would be at our disposal.

Deano turned to me and held out a key with a small amount of white powder on the tip.

'Here,' he motioned.

I thanked him and swiftly hoovered it up.

'What's the plan for tonight, then?' Enya inquired, tapping her foot on the carpet in time with the music and lighting the joint.

'We're celebrating.' Lauryn informed her.

'Celebrating what?'

'Freedom. Unemployment. Being single. The summer...' I began rhyming off my reasons.

'So our lives in general then?' She grinned as she began fiddling with the tuning on the speakers again.

'Hey, I have a job.' Lauryn protested.

'And the rest of us are students.' Deano pointed out.

'So, it's just you then...Awkward.' Enya raised an eyebrow and I looked at her blankly. 'I'm only jokng.' She reached over and squeezed my arm with a smile.

'Great!' I exhaled.

'Don't be silly, we're all very supportive of your plan for self-destruction.' Deano assured me.

'It's not a plan for...whatever. But there are conditions.' I started.

Deano sniggered to himself. I ignored him and sniffed repeatedly in an attempt to control my stuffy nose.

'Such as?' Enya puffed on her spliff and waved away bits of ash that were flying everywhere.

'Well,' I said, 'you have to agree to being filmed, by Lauryn, throughout the duration of the operation.' Lauryn nodded in agreement, 'And you have to be open to experimentation.'

'Right...' Enya eyed me curiously.

'Oh, and you have to take part in at least one of the things on my bucket list.'

'Bucket list?'

'Don't ask.' Deano shook his head.

'Fair enough.'

'Hey, where's Cian?' He asked her, taking a key before twisting open his bottle of cider and gulping back half of it in one go.

'He's gone to meet one of the guys he does PR with for Johnny's events, Jamie. They said they'd be coming over here after.' Enya replied as she maneuvered from the sofa to a cross-legged positon on the rug. I watched her stub out a half-smoked joint, her finger nails bitten down and yellowish at the tips.

'Never heard of him,' Deano shrugged.

'He's funny, you'll like him.'

'Well, as long as he's prepared.' He winked at Enya.

'What are you winking at people for?' I queried, suspicious.

'Well, I happened to have acquired something that may be of interest to you,' he said with a half-attempted air of mystery.

'A sense of humour?'

'No, actually.' Deano reached into his jacket pocket and pulled out a clear bag of pills. 'Try, Blue Roses.'

'Blue?..No! Are you serious?' I shrieked in excitement.

'Yup.' he grinned. 'Turns out there are dark corners of the internet where you can not only find them, but have them delivered straight to your front door.'

'Let me see.' Lauryn reached out and grabbed the bag out of Deano's hand.

'Alright, calm down.' He took another swig of cider. Lauryn and I jumped up immediately and surveyed the bag under the dim living room light. Six little purple-blue pills shaped like roses. They had been sold as herbal highs in various alternative shops in town up until the summer. But when the powers that be had discovered that they were in fact more powerful than your average ecstasy hit off the street, they'd been whisked off the shelves and had been notoriously difficult to obtain ever since. I had to say I was rather impressed with Deano's efforts. He sat back looking rather chuffed with himself.

'They're so pretty,' Lauryn sighed.

'And strong,' warned Enya 'So don't enjoy them too much. You'll just want more.'

'Okay, oh Wise One.' Deano joked.

'You're a wicked pill-pushing magician,' I planted a kiss on Deano's forehead and Lauryn and I did a little celebration dance, fist-pumping and jumping around the others. Enya and Deano shook their heads at us as if we were their unruly children. We were that giddy we almost didn't hear the knock on the front door.

Enya jumped up. 'I'll get it.'

CHAPTER 3

I heard Cian curse the weather as he shuffled in from the rain.

'Alright, you wreck-head. Trust it to be raining in June,' Enya motioned him inside, followed by a second figure. 'That's Northern Ireland for you. Guys, this is Jamie.'

I looked round and my eyes fixed on him. For a moment I almost had to catch my breath. He reached out his hand and the corner of his mouth curled into the hint of a smile, his icy blue eyes penetrating mine confidently. There was no wavering in his gaze, yet it was soft and tantalizing, and for a moment I was entrapped. He was beautiful. I felt the trickle of electricity seep from my neck down to the small of my back, and like a magnet my hand went to meet his.

'Hi, I'm Scarlet.' I tried to sound cool and indifferent, and I'm pretty sure I succeeded.

'Nice to meet you.' he said.

I suddenly felt exposed, and only allowed his eyes to linger on mine for a moment longer. When he spoke, the music dulled and the room softened into an obscure haze, as if the world had slowed down just to hear it. His energy was palpable. Instinctively I smiled, inviting it in for a second before he broke his gaze and turned to the others. Mildly unsettled, although not really knowing why, I made a point of acknowledging Cian before the pair began cracking open beers and lighting cigarettes.

'Thanks for the invite,' Jamie winked at Enya and threw her a can, the playful smile surfacing again.

'You're more than welcome.' I detected a hint of shyness in her voice, which was unusual for Enya. Apparently I wasn't the only one he made nervous.

Almost immediately, Jamie took center stage. He was one of those frustratingly confident people that could get away with it because he exuded just the right amount, with a hint of arrogance that intrigued rather than repelled. I watched enthralled as he delighted Enya and Lauryn with stories of bumping into their favourite indie bands backstage at the summer festivals.

'I'll see about getting you tickets to next year's gig.' He said casually.

'Really?' Lauryn's eyes lit up.

'Yeah, shouldn't be a problem.'

Deano looked nonchalant, and turned talk to the Blue Roses, passing them to Cian and Jamie for inspection as if he was showing off his prize cow at a cattle market. He declined their offer of cash towards their share.

'Next one's on me, then,' Cian said, tossing him a beer.

'The trick with these,' Jamie mused, flipping one of the pills in the air and catching it expertly in his mouth, 'is to ride the wave. Let it build naturally without thinking too much about it, and when it peaks, it'll blow your head off.'

'You've had them before?' Deano asked, surprised.

'Herbals aren't hard to come across when you work in a bar.'

'I see.'

I could feel his eyes on me now. Tentatively surveying my face, neck, shoulders, until I shivered inside. We hadn't even swallowed the bloody pills yet and I already felt a buzz simmering in the pit of my stomach, anticipation bubbling in my throat. No one had ever looked at me like that before. I presumed there wasn't a girl in the world who hadn't fallen for it. He would glance at me intently for a moment, then away again just as quickly, leaving me wondering if I had imagined it. He knew exactly what he was doing, and he did it with ease.

'What about you?'

'Me?' I asked.

'Yeah, ever had these before?'

'Um...no, not these. I hear they're good though.' I looked down and started twiddling the bottle top of my wine.

'A Roses virgin then. Don't worry, I'll look after you.' I raised an eyebrow but couldn't help smiling to myself. He threw the bag of pills to me, 'Come on you lot, don't let me get winged out by myself.'

I passed the bag around, a modern day pass-the-parcel.

'Wait!' Lauryn squealed, launching herself across the carpet to where she'd left her rucksack.

'What the..?' Deano frowned.

She pulled out her camcorder, and flicked it open.

'Almost forgot.'

'Are you really going to video us?' he asked.

'Yup. You'll forget it's even there after a while.'

'I don't want to end up on YouTube,' he huffed.

'Deano, it's *art.*'

He shrugged as she pointed the camera down at the pill in her other hand and demonstrated her best muffled space-cadet voice.

'Three seconds to lift off, Commander come in.'

'Affirmative. 3, 2, 1...' Cian replied as we washed down the Roses with a few swigs of beer.

'Intergalactic space station, here we come.' Enya declared, saluting us all in military fashion.

Jamie grinned. 'No going back now.'

'It's the perfect means of escapism without having to leave your house. Budget holidaying for the masses.' Enya mused.

'I just want to get away full stop.' I thought aloud.

Jamie glanced at me before leaning down to where I sat on the carpet and resting on his right arm.

'Where would you go?' he asked, the closeness of his skin to mine making me uneasy. When he spoke it was as if he used a special tone just for me, quieter. My eyes darted around the room to avoid having to look right at him.

'Um, I don't know.' I said, 'Somewhere hot.'

'Can I come with you?'

'If you like.' I let out a tiny laugh and could have punched myself in the face for acting like such a moron.

'Maybe we can all go next year.' Lauryn smiled at me.

'Yeah, like in a villa...by the beach...with loads of coke...' I sighed contentedly.

'I hate water.' Deano remarked.

'You hate everything.' I said.

We were all fidgeting about apprehensively waiting to feel the effects of the pills. It was like that excited nervousness you get right before a first date but way better.

'Is anything happening yet?' Lauryn asked impatiently, 'I don't think they're working.'

'Relax, give it time.' Enya assured her.

'Do you feel anything?' Lauryn frowned and turned to me.

'I don't think so.' I said.

'You're overthinking it. When it hits you, you'll know about it.' Jamie promised.

Between the hum of voices and the mellow house beats in the background, conversations began to overlap and time became obscure. I wasn't sure whether it had been a few minutes or a few hours before the warm tingling spread across my shoulders and filtered down my arms. I watched Jamie, unable to keep my eyes off him. He seemed happy to do the entertaining, so for once I shut up and let his energy envelop the room. Lauryn chattered away with Cian about her latest film project, while Enya rolled another joint and announced her plans to start selling T-shirts that she'd designed herself at college. All of us except Deano had somehow ended up in a cluster on the carpet, and suddenly I looked up at Jamie. He began to smile, excited yet with a surprising hint of uncertainty, as if we both knew something intensely special was coming. Already I could feel my skin, bones, and every other fiber of my being succumb to imminent bliss in a steady but certain ascend as the chemicals filtered into our blood streams. We all felt it in sync, and our tangible energies seemed to fuse to create one magical vibration. Suddenly we were drenched in a beautiful, euphoric glow, and there was no mistaking it.

'Holy shit.' Deano breathed, sinking down off the sofa to join our little oasis on the floor.

'I know.' I murmured.

'How come we always end up on the floor?' Enya queried, resting her head contentedly on Cian's shoulder.

'Because it's a circle of love, invisible to the naked eye.' Lauryn grinned.

'Well if we keep returning to the love circle, we should just get rid of the sofas and make more room.'

'It's a circle of love, not a love circle.' I interjected.

'What's the difference?'

'Well, love circle sounds like an orgy. Or a euphemism for lady parts.'

Enya frowned.

'You can keep me well out of your love circle, thank you very much.'

Lauryn and I fell about giggling. Instantly I could sense Jamie glance at me. I didn't want to meet his eye, I knew if I did I might get drawn in to a place I didn't know the way out of. Every time I went to speak to him, I stopped, instead lighting a cigarette. I must have smoked twenty already. I suddenly realised I'd only had about three lines of coke in the past few hours, an unusually small amount under the circumstances. Cian and Lauryn began bickering over the music on the laptop, but ended up just laughing and hugging each other. The Roses had well and truly kicked in.

'Pass it here,' Jamie said, extracting it from between their clumsy embrace. In moments, the room was filled with the sensual sounds of deep trance.

'Listen.' Jamie held a hand in the air and gestured for us all to be silent, 'Just listen.'

We felt the music pulsate through each of us, delicately but with a clear destination. It was as if the song had been personally made for us, the soundtrack to our climactic journey towards inevitable bliss. Surely it didn't get better than this?

I lay back and rested my head on a faded blue and pink cushion, adorned with gold and silver beads that formed a shimmering, heavenly halo. I spent a good ten minutes absorbing the almost overwhelming ecstasy that had spread through my veins. I studied the swirly patterns and delicate creases of fabric on our homemade curtains,which had always seemed so bland before. The entire room was dimly bathed in a warm, pink light that revealed looming shapes and shadows on the ceiling. It all seemed so perfect and safe and warm. I laughed quietly to myself. You know you're wiped out when the decor brings a tear to your eye.

'What's funny?'

I hadn't even noticed Jamie lay his head down next to mine. I turned to him and smiled, a newfound ease making me feel connected to everyone in the room, especially him.

'The curtains.'

'Oh, the curtains. Of course.'

'I think this is nirvana.'

'It's pretty amazing, I'm not gonna lie.' He handed me a cigarette. 'I feel like I've been launched into a parallel universe.'

'That's exactly what it is, a parallel universe. There is nothing higher than this. I was thinking I was the only one who'd arrived here.'

'Nope, we're all here,' he laughed and I ran my eyes over his features, which seemed nothing short of perfect right at that moment.

'Have we gone mad?' I asked dreamily.

'Probably. But I wouldn't have it any other way.' Deano's voice came from somewhere behind us.

'I never want to go home,' Lauryn sighed, laying down beside us and curling her fingers around mine.

'I love you Lollipop.' I told her fondly.

'I love you more, Scarly.' she said, 'This is what heaven is,' she paused and turned the video camera towards me, 'Everyone should know about this.' she looked at me, her face serious.

'It's ok,' I laughed, squeezing her hand in reassurance, 'We'll tell them.'

'It's like we were all meant to be here. Right now, like this.'

I nodded in agreement. She didn't even have to speak, we all felt it. An incredible rush of emotion that tied us together and made you just want to explode with pleasure.

'Seems that way,' Jamie said quietly. He closed his eyes and began humming along to the music. I watched him tapping out the rhythm contentedly on his chest.

'You're beautiful,' I whispered.

'So are you.' He kept his eyes closed for a few moments, and then looked up at the ceiling, apparently immersed in thought.

We didn't speak for several minutes, our words hanging softly in the air. The delectably gorgeous atmosphere seemed to lull gently in time with our breathing, rising and falling in perfect sync. We were being serenaded by the Roses, expertly twirled and swayed lovingly to their peaceful music. Something magical was happening, and the intense, pure love that filled the air around us made it seem impossible to ever feel worried or sad again. As Jamie leaned over to change the song on the laptop his hand gently rested on the small of my back and it felt perfect.

'We're in some sort of cocoon in here,' Lauryn said, 'all warm and safe. How are we supposed to go out and be normal after this?'

'Trust me,' Enya grinned, 'Once it wears off you'll want to hide for a few days, but then you'll be right as rain again.'

I couldn't soak up enough of that feeling, my fingers and toes literally buzzed with serotonin.

'If I lose my mind tonight, I'm glad it's with you guys.' I said.

'Cheers to that.' Deano raised his cider bottle and we all toasted our weird journey to the other side.

'This is what I wanted, Deano,' I said to him, 'Real freedom, away from everything else. People are so busy running around trying to follow all the rules that they've forgotten what life's really about. It terrifies me that I might end up like them if I'm not careful.'

'I don't think you have to worry about that,' he smiled at me from beneath his thick eyebrows that I always tried to pluck but he'd never let me. 'But reality's always going to be there, unfortunately. Whether we like it or not.'

'Why can't this be our reality?'

He said nothing, his brow furrowed pensively.

I listened to the music for a moment and lit a cigarette. Jamie was beside me, still in his own world. I smiled at how content he looked, when suddenly he looked at me.

'Do you want to get some fresh air?'

It took me a minute to realise he was talking to me and I automatically nodded. He probably could have asked me to do anything right then and there and I would have agreed. Lauryn looked at me knowingly.

'Have fun.' she said.

I rolled my eyes. You could always rely on your best friend to make a situation wonderfully awkward for you. Luckily, right then, I didn't care. Nothing mattered.

The rain had stopped. Jamie and I sat closely on the front garden bench and the night's chill felt fresh against my skin. I looked up at the inky sky, stars dotted sporadically across a huge black canvas. For a moment we basked in its vastness and just listened to the sound of our breathing.

'It's nice to take a break away from everyone, to enjoy it on your own. You know?'

His voice danced on the air like a smooth stone skimming a lake.

'I'm so fucking content. I don't want for anything right now other than for everything to be exactly the way it is. Does that make any sense?' I let the words pour out unashamedly and laughed at the sky.

He smiled. 'It does.'

I felt the warmth of him at my side, and yet another surge of happiness course through me until I felt like bursting.

'I guess we wouldn't take this stuff if it didn't make us feel amazing,' he continued, his breath dissipating in the night air, 'Problem is, we're human. We always want more.'

'Not right now. This is perfect.' I said.

I noticed my hands were quivering slightly, I wasn't sure if it was the Roses vibrating my insides, or being out here with him, just the two of us.

'It'll be a different story tomorrow, when it wears off.' he laughed.

'I hope I don't forget all this. Like, what if it all becomes like a dream that I can't remember properly? I've never felt anything like this, it's too special to forget.'

'You'll remember. Especially after a big come-down.' he smiled at me.

'Can we not talk about coming down,' I shook my head as a vague hint of anxiety arose inside me, 'I don't want to think about it.'

'Ok, no more come-down talk.'

He took my hand in his, the warmth enveloping my fingers and spreading through every inch of my body. He looked at me steadily, and this time I didn't look away. I knew I was being drawn in, losing myself in the achingly beautiful mess of it. I was his, completely and irrevocably, and he already knew it. What was left of my rational mind sighed in frustration, but the rest was too intoxicated to care.

As he reached up and pulled my face to his, any remnants of hesitation melted away. His lips pressed hard against mine and he kissed me like he'd been waiting forever. I clutched his jacket and pulled him close, consumed by the magic. I wanted to absorb every part of him, to succumb to the heart-stopping desire that overwhelmed and left me breathless. I could have stayed like that for an age, and it would't have been enough. Time had warped and slowed, and when he gently let his hand fall from my cheek, his lips brushed lightly on mine and lingered for a moment.

'Oi, love birds.' Cian's voice penetrated the darkness.

I looked round and found him emerging from the shadows, grinning from ear to ear.

'Sorry to interrupt, Enya's going to play some guitar. They want you both to join us instead of eating each other's faces out here.'

'Nice way to put it.' I said, reluctantly pulling myself away from Jamie.

'You make a lovely couple,' he teased.

'Give it a rest, Cian,' Jamie stood up and lit a cigarette.

'Nicer than that last melter, anyway.'

'Don't start badmouthing Amber, mate.

I stiffened. 'Amber who?'

'McDowell.' Jamie paused awkwardly, as if the words had slipped out of his mouth.

'As in Luke McDowell's sister?'

'Yeah....you know Luke?'

'I used to go out with him, we broke up a few weeks ago.'

I could feel Jamie tense.

'Lucky you.'Cian muttered sarcastically.

I looked at Jamie, confused.

'We never got on,' he explained. 'Forget it, it was ages ago. Cian, tell them we'll be in in a minute.'

He held out his hand. A part of me wanted to ask why, but another held back. Right now, it didn't matter and as I felt the warmth of his fingers in mine my anxiety quickly dissipated.

'Can I tell you a secret?' he said, lowering his voice.

'What?' I paused as we reached the front door.

'I've never really taken those Roses before.'

I looked up at him.

'But...why did you say you had?' I asked, bewildered.

'Because,' his eyes sparkled and I lost myself in them again, 'Everyone enjoys it more if they think there's someone there who's done it before, and they trust you. No one freaks out. You've got to know how to tame your audience and make them feel comfortable.'

I shook my head with a laugh, unsure whether it was manipulative or simply genius. Then I leaned in and kissed him lightly on the lips.

'How did you come up with that trick?'

He shrugged and then winked as he opened the door for me and led me in to join the others. 'I just know how people work.'

I smiled as I felt his fingers in mine and followed him

inside.'You're pretty amazing, aren't you?'

Chapter 4

Mid-afternoon light crept through a gap in the curtains casting a harsh line across my face. I frowned and felt my fingers twitch. With effort I managed to roll over and Lauryn's fluffy mop tickled the end of my nose. I could feel the steady rise and fall of Deano's breath on the other side of me and gradually became aware of my surroundings. It took a few minutes to recall how I'd came to be squished in the middle of them. I knew We'd been awake for around two days or so before eventually making it upstairs and falling asleep in a heap.

Eventually I pulled myself up and instinctively felt around the bed for a cigarette. I was utterly drained, my arms heavy and my face aching from where I'd chewed my jaw for twelve hours straight. But while most of the chemicals had left me physically, a faint tingling sense of anticipation remained, reminding me of our incredible night. I smiled dreamily before locating my handbag somewhere near Deano's feet and rummaging around with the eagerness of a child on Christmas morning. I found my phone and my heart began pumping. Two new messages.

Had a great night. Hope to see you soon. J x

I sighed inwardly as relief washed over me. I was scared for a moment that I'd thought him up, that the whole thing was an illusion fabricated by my own wiped-out mind. Recollections began to accumulate in my mind like fragments of a dream. All of us dancing in the living room while she strummed the guitar, Jamie's hand around my waist, the colours rich and vibrating with energy. And then resting my head in his lap as we sang and talked into the early hours, soaking up as much of the ambiance as possible before we had to leave our perfect universe and return to earth. Now the walls, the floor, the wooden chair in the corner, became hard and grey. Dulled, like watery paint. I expected the living room looked something like a tomb, a bleak reminder of what had been.

I opened the second text. It was a group message from Johnny, Jamie's boss.

> This Friday, DJ Orta blesses us all with his electro-house mix, followed by Amy L on the decks till 5am, killing it with heavenly trance anthems. BYOB, location TBC by text message on Friday morning. Doors open 11pm, £5 in. Keep it discreet, kids.

A muffled groan behind me broke the silence.

'Pass me a cigarette, Scarlet.' Lauryn mumbled. I found two in my bag and passed her one, nestling back down in my warm spot between her and Deano.

'My face hurts.' I told her.

'Join the club.'

'What day is it?'

She thought for a moment. 'Monday, I think.'

'Jesus.'

'I know. I had to call work a few hours ago and tell them I had the flu. Worth it though.' she said, her face brightening.

'Definitely. Although I literally feel like I traveled through time and space, I'm bloody exhausted.'

She sighed in agreement, the smudged remains of eyeliner making her look like she'd just come out of a boxing ring.

'You know what would make us feel a gazillion times better?'

I found the left-over half gram of coke in my jacket pocket. The Roses had been so good that I'd forgotten to hoover up the rest of my gear.

'Don't go racking up without me, you greedy bastards.' A muffled voice came from under Deano's pillow.

'As if I would.'

I quickly cut three even lines and licked the crummy remnants off the edge of my bank card, shuddering at the taste. We snorted them all in quick succession and collapsed back down into bed.

'Better than Weetabix.' I said, feeling instantly rejuvenated.

'Coke for breakfast.' Deano tutted.

'Don't you start.' I grinned.

I told them both about Johnny's rave on Friday night.

'I'll go, as long as I make at least one lecture this week.' Deano said, stretching his arms above his head and sniffing his armpit, 'I need a shower.'

'I think we all do,' I peered down at my wine-stained skirt and curled my lip in disgust. 'Gross.'

'Jamie will be there, he works for Johnny, doesn't he?' Lauryn remarked, poking me hard in the ribs.

I tried to conceal a smile but quickly caved.

'Isn't he class.' I squeaked.

'He's pretty funny, and it's so obvious you like him.'

'Oh shit. Like, really desperate obvious?' I stared at her, horrified.

'Erm...no, not really-'

'You look at him like he's some kind of God.' Deano interrupted. I turned round and glared at him.

'No, I do not.'

'Yeah, you do,'

'I think you forget I was on pills as well. I'm pretty sure I was in love with the lamp that night.' I knew it wasn't entirely true, but I didn't want him to know it.

'Whatever,' he shrugged, 'he just seems like a bit of a prick.'

'Why? He was perfectly nice to you all night.' I couldn't conceal the surprise on my face. Deano didn't particularly like anyone much, but I didn't expect such a strong reaction.

'I don't know. I just don't really trust him.'

‘Well it’s really none of your business.’ I said, irritated.

‘Don’t be so defensive.’

Lauryn squirmed uncomfortably.

‘I should really get my work clothes ready.’ She jumped up from the bed.

‘Yeah, I’ve got an assignment to finish.’ Deano said as he got up and pulled on a pair of socks.

Trust him to shit all over my parade. Clash of male egos most likely. Deano could huff all he wanted, he’d get over it soon. I pulled the covers up around my neck and re-read Jamie’s text. That delicious high returned as I remembered his hand on the back of my neck, that playful look in his eyes that was both dangerous and irresistible. He was my ultimate hit. All I knew was I needed more.

*

My finger tapped impatiently on the hand rail as the rattling bus slowed to a halt. They always seemed to take forever, especially when you wanted to get somewhere. I jumped off and walked briskly through a small crowd at the bus stop, Lauryn practically jogging to keep up with me.

‘Okay, it’s down here. Past the junction, first left onto Rugby Road, then second right. Apparently.’ I instructed her.

‘Are you sure it’s not second left?’ she stepped in line with me and fumbled with the Sat Nav on her phone.

'No, it's first left.'

She scrunched up her brow and examined the screen. I wanted to get to the dealer's house before dark. It was already getting late, the rich summer sun fading into the evening.

'Why don't we just go to the usual guy?' Lauryn asked as we expertly dodged our way around pedestrians. Summer seemed to make people emerge from their homes and run around like rats in a maze.

'Be*cause*,' I said, 'he's on holiday and Deano said we should try this guy's stuff because it's better. He can't collect it because he has an assignment to finish.'

'Oh...junction!' she screeched triumphantly.

I'd actually seen it about a minute ago but I didn't tell her.

'Okay, we're not far - '

'Wait for the green...Scarlet!' she yanked my sleeve as I shot across the road, an angry lorry driver beeping in fury.

'He was miles away from me! If you wait at a roundabout for the green man you'll be waiting all bloody day.' I reasoned.

'You should be careful.'

'Don't worry. I can't die. I'm Wonder Woman.'

She shook her head and I laughed. We power-walked left down a row of terraced houses before reaching a dead end. I frowned.

'That can't be right.' I muttered.

'I think it's second left.' Lauryn said.

I paused.

'Just follow me.' I instructed as I marched back up the street and out onto the main road. As we reached the next left Lauryn piped up again.

'See? Rugby Road. Second left.' she said with a hint of satisfaction.

I ignored her muffled sniggers as we headed down the road and then turned right onto the correct street.

'There, number 29.' Lauryn pointed to a faded blue door and I squinted to make out the numbers. The front of the house looked like it needed a good scrub, white paint peeling off the brickwork and mossy green stuff crawling out of the cracks.

'Okay, I'll go first.'

I wasn't quite as hasty now. It was always a bit unsettling going into a drug dealer's personal space, especially one you hadn't met before. That was all part of the fun, though. I looked at the shiny black BMW parked on the curb, and wondered why this guy couldn't spend a little of his mega bucks on making his home a bit more presentable. It was often the way with these types, nice cars and crummy houses you wouldn't want to stick around in for too long. As I pushed the buzzer Lauryn shifted uneasily behind me, looking over her shoulder down the street and back again.

'You couldn't make it any more obvious, could you?' I hissed.

'Wha - Oh, sorry.' she whispered.

I rolled my eyes. I know Lauryn hated doing this, but she could at least try to appear inconspicuous. There was movement in the house and I stood up straight, my friendly-user-meeting-dealer face at the ready. Suddenly the door swung open and a grubby twenty-something guy with long, straggly hair and what can only be described as a wizard's beard stared at me suspiciously.

'Hi! I'm Scarlet. We're looking for Dave?'

He eyed me for a moment and frowned.

'Are you Deano's mates?' his voice was gravelly and solemn, like he was bringing us in to a morgue.

'Yep, that's right.' I said, way too cheerfully.

Then, with what seemed like a colossal effort, he opened the door and waved us towards the stairs.

'First room at the top.' he mumbled behind that greasy mass of unnecessary facial hair.

'Sweet, thank you.' I smiled.

As we climbed the carpet-less stairs, the smell of stale cigarettes, weed and what I think was wet dog filled my nostrils and made me want to gag. The atmosphere wasn't exactly welcoming, but I trusted Deano. Lauryn stayed right beside me and I realised Greasy Beard was following close behind. In hindsight I probably should have knocked before going in but didn't really think. It took a few minutes before I could even see through the smoke in the room. The curtains were closed and the only light came from a dull table lamp in the corner. It was like a bloody bat cave. I spotted a man, who was quite clearly Dave, slumped in an armchair beside the bed looking like a poor man's Pablo Escobar.

He had that self-entitled look about him, as if he was a man to be respected. My arse. But you had to play the game with these guys, or you'd end up in a sticky situation. Another dirty guy with a mess of curly hair and the spindliest arms I've ever seen was hunched over cross-legged on the bed bashing away at an Xbox controller. He didn't even look up. Greasy Beard strode past us and plonked himself down on the bed beside Curly Head and began to roll a joint. Dave nodded at us and I didn't know whether he was saying hello or wanted us to sit down.

' 'Much you after?' He sounded just as disinterested as the greasy wizard, which was a bit of a cheek considering I was a customer.

'Two g's, please.'

He didn't move from the faded old armchair and I kind of stood there for a minute awkwardly chewing my lip. What a pleasant group of humans. Lauryn stood slightly behind me, her eyes darting around the room like a frightened deer. I tried to relax my posture hoping she'd follow suit, but we just ended up looking more uncomfortable. She was never very good at this stuff, I was usually the one who had to gabble my way out of situations. Dave lit a cigarette and I felt his eyes look me up and down slowly as he flicked ash onto the floor. *Creep, just give me the fucking gear.*

'Here.'

To my relief, he finally reached into his shirt pocket and held out two tiny bags. His fingernails were full of dirt so I swiftly grabbed them off him to avoid catching some form of hepatitis.

'Hundred an' twenty.' he said.

My shoulders tensed again as I pulled out the notes from my back pocket.

'Erm, Deano said one hundred. Fifty each.'

Well that sure got his attention.

'You get what you pay for. That's quality stuff. Sixty each.'

Sixty quid? For a bit of coke mixed with baking soda? My stomach twisted anxiously.

'Well, see, there must have been a mix up. I'm sure it's great stuff, it's just we only have one hundred.'

This time the other two looked at us, surrounded in the middle of their dingy bat cave like lion's prey.

'You think I'm a mug?' Dave growled, his voice getting louder.

'No, not at all. It's just -'

'One twenty or fuck off. I haven't got time for this.'

'Let's just go, Scarlet.' Lauryn squeaked.

'Hold on.' I waved my hand at her dismissively.

Like heck was I going anywhere without that coke. I racked my brains and searched in my handbag for any stray notes before I spotted something. I fiddled with the clasp of the bracelet on my wrist.

'What are you-?'

'Shh, Lauryn.' I managed to release the clasp and dangled it in front of Dave the Dick, 'Here, take this, too. It's a Pandora bracelet with charms. It's worth about a hundred.'

'Didn't your Mum give - ' Lauryn started.

'It's fine. I don't care.'

I just wanted to get out of there and away from the miserable bastards. They could have my damn knickers if it shut them up. Dave the Dick scowled before leaning out of his shabby throne and yanking the bracelet off me and holding it up for inspection. It was the real thing so he couldn't really complain. Eventually he shoved it into his pocket.

'Fine. Give me the hundred.' He sighed as if he'd done us some huge favour.

I didn't want to piss him off anymore at that stage so said my thanks and quickly made for the door. As we hurriedly clambered down the stairs and out the front I breathed a sigh of relief. We scuttled down the path in silence until we reached the end of the street. Then I looked at Lauryn and burst out laughing.

'Your face.' I cackled, lighting a cigarette. Her expression was nothing short of distraught.

'Jesus, Scarlet.'

'Oh come on, it was only a stupid bracelet. It's kind of funny when you think about it.'

The cool evening had settled and I wrapped my cardigan around my shoulders.

'No, it isn't.' she said crossly.

I glanced at her and a smile crept across my face. Being angry just didn't suit her, she looked like a child who's had their sweets taken off them.

'I'm sorry. Don't worry, we won't go back there.' She looked at me and her face softened. I put my arm around her shoulders as we dawdled back to the bus stop. 'Let's see if this gear is as good as it's cracked up to be. I'll do you out a big fat one.'

That would have been all well and good had we been able to find a toilet to rack up lines in. Eventually we spotted a pub

The pair of us squeezed into one cubicle and I poured a few rocks out of one of the bags onto the toilet lid. I laid a piece a paper on top and scraped over it vigorously to break the powder down into as much as possible, and soon had two neat rows lined up.

'How is it?' I urged as Lauryn rolled up the piece of paper and took hers.

'Good.' She scrunched up her nose and nodded.

Just as I bent down to hoover up mine a booming Jamaican voice bellowed from outside the door.

'Only wan atta time! Ya hear? Wan!' The cleaner banged her fist on the door, 'I'm nat stupid woman! Come atta der!'

Lauryn looked at me wide-eyed and we scrambled to put everything away.

'Oh, sorry!' I called, 'Two seconds.'

She banged on the door again as I snorted the line with much less discretion than I'd hoped for.

'Outta der! Ya hear?'

'Alright!' I shouted between muffled giggles.

I brushed the lid for any remnants and opened the door to see her glaring at us over thin-rimmed glasses. She muttered and cursed as we made our way out, shaking her head.

'Christ, how many obstacles do you have to go through for a few lines?' I laughed as we strolled outside.

'Well, I'm never going back there again.'

'To Dave the Dick?'

'His room smelled like feet.' She wrinkled her nose.

'I bet that other guy's beard smelled even worse.' We both shuddered in disgust.

I could relax on the journey home. As the bus shuddered off towards home I looked down at my bare wrist and felt a twinge of guilt. Mum had bought it for my birthday last year. But I quickly pushed it out of my mind, it was only a material thing. I may be returning home minus a piece of jewellery but I had two little bags of joy in my pocket that would more than compensate for it.

Of course, by the next day the coke was long gone. I looked at my bare wrist now and was pissed off. No bracelet and no coke. I'd also have to figure out an excuse for when Mum found out it was gone. With my mood flat and my mind restless, I pottered around the flat until Deano emerged about midday, his arms full

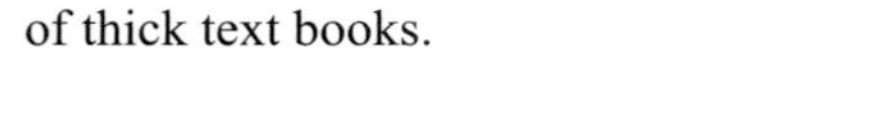

of thick text books.

'What are you doing?' I asked curiously.

'Revising. Why?'

'I thought the term was over?'

'I have one more exam.'

'Oh,' I scuffed my shoes against the skirting board, 'I'm bored. Lauryn's working.'

'Maybe you should do something productive.' He said disinterestedly.

He packed the books into a black backpack and heaved it onto his back.

'Where are you going?' I pried.

'To the park.'

'Which one?'

'Botanic'

'Can I come?'

He did his standard huffing for a minute.

'Fine. As long as you be quiet and let me study.'

It was so hot and crowded on the bus that I started to regret my decision. Why was the public transport experience always so grim? When we reached the park it was packed. The Northern

Irish, typical as ever, saw a few rays of sunshine and were out sunbathing in full force. Deano found a patch in the shade under a big old willow tree and dumped his bag on the grass.

'Wow, it's hotter than I thought.' I said as I lay my jacket on the ground as a make-shift towel.

'Too good to sit inside.' Deano said, peering across the vast green at groups of people lazing idly.

'Can I have a fag, please?' I looked at him pleadingly.

'What happened to the pack you had yesterday?'

'I smoked them.'

'For god' s sake. Here.'

He chucked his tobacco pouch in my direction before settling into position and opening one of those big boring books. I opened a can of Coke and it hissed loudly as the bubbles escaped. I glugged down half the can in one go.

'Want some?' I held out the can to Deano.

'Nope.' He didn't look up from his book.

I began to hum the tune to a song I'd heard on the shower radio that morning, sipping from the can and taking in my surroundings.

'Not like you to turn down coke.' I smirked.

'Funny.' he replied, unamused.

He still didn't take his eyes off the text book, not even when he reached into his backpack and pulled out a bottle half-full with water. He sipped the rest of it slowly and eventually got up to throw it in the bin.

'Take this.'

I held the empty can of Coke out to him and when he returned I lay back and soaked up the warm air.

'So why do you hate Jamie?'

'What?' Deano pretended he hadn't heard me.

'You heard.'

'I don't *hate* him,' he looked up from his book, 'I just don't particularly like him.'

'Why?'

'Just, because.'

'Because why?'

'*Because*. Am I not allowed to not like someone?'

'Well, I think he's great.' I said matter-of-factly.

'I can see that.'

We were silent for a few moments and I heard people laughing loudly as they flung a tennis ball towards a brown labrador, who caught it expertly in his mouth.

'Just be careful. I don't want you to get hurt, that's all.' he mumbled.

Deano never felt comfortable talking about his emotions. I smiled. He cared in his own funny little way.

'I know. You don't have to worry.' I glanced at him out of the corner of my eye, 'Moody prick.'

I saw the hint of a smirk beneath his beard and I knew things were okay between us.

'God I wish I had actual coke.' I grumbled, changing the subject as I leaned on my arms and tilted my head back to look up at the few wisps of white cloud.

'Well, I've only got enough left for tomorrow night.' Deano said firmly, reaching into his back pocket, 'So it's not going anywhere.'

'Fine.' I scowled.

He ignored me for a second, then a frown formed on his forehead.

'What's wrong?' I asked as he scrambled around in his jeans pockets.

'It's...hold on...Oh, fuck.'

'What?' I sat up.

'I've lost a gram.'

'Of coke?' I cried.

'Shh! No, of sugar, what do you think?'

'Oh, shit.' I stared at him, open-mouthed.

'It was right here, in this pocket.' he said, bewildered, as he patted down every inch of his jeans.

'Well, where could it have gone?' I asked.

'I don't know.'

Deano began rummaging around in his bag, throwing bits of paper and pens out of it as he went.

'That really sucks,' I empathised, 'Happened to me once.'

'Help me look for it,' he urged, 'I had it when I left the house, it can't be far.'

He crawled around under the tree, inspecting the grass like one of those sniffer dogs.

'It's probably long gone.' I said, peering around at the huge expanse of grass around us. He probably lost it on the bus, in which case it was definitely history.

'Just help me, will you?'

I sighed and and made a feeble attempt at tracing over the grass with my hands to find it.

'If you help me look, I'll give you a couple of lines out of it.' he promised.

Instantly I was on my feet.

'It must be here somewhere.' I insisted.

I joined him on the ground, crawling around the tree like two people escaped from the mental hospital.

'Check over by the bin, you walked over that way.' I said.

We widened our search area, crouching down to scan every patch of grass. A few people were looking now. I didn't care, I just wanted to find it so I could have a line. Deano turned his pockets inside out for a fourth time and I scurried around on my knees until there were big round grass stains on them.

'Oh, for fuck's sake.' I whined, trying to brush my jeans down before heading over to Deano to join him on all fours under the tree again.

'Are you sure it's not in your - ?'

'Alright there, guys?' My words caught in my mouth as we both turned our heads and looked up at the park warden, 'Looking for something?'

He was a middle-aged man with a short, graying beard. His uniform was spotless and he wore his badge as if it were an army stripe, his chest all puffed out and proud.

'Um...no, we were just...er...' Deano stuttered.

'Earring.' I declared.

'Pardon?' the warden said.

'We're looking for an earring.'

I looked at Deano and he nodded in agreement.

‘Yes, that’s right,’ he said, ‘We lost an earring.’

The warden eyed us skeptically for a moment.

‘Must be valuable, then?’ he raised an eyebrow.

‘Yes, very valuable. Gold, in fact. I got them for Christmas and they’re worth quite a bit.’ I gabbled.

‘Well, in that case,’ the warden bent over slightly and began surveying the ground around us, ‘I’ll help you look.’

Deano and I gawked in horror.

‘It’s really okay...’ Deano insisted.

‘I don’t mind giving you a hand. Not much else to do around here. Now, where did you last have it?’ he persisted.

‘Eh...I’m not sure...’ I pretended to look around for the imaginary earring, praying that he wouldn’t find the gram.

‘Looks like it’s gone. Oh, well.’ Deano shrugged.

‘Yep, it’s really not worth *that* much.’ I said.

The warden eventually stood upright and shook his head.

‘Sorry, kids. No sign of it here. Perhaps you’ll find it at home.’

‘That’s ok. Thanks anyway.’ I said.

‘Yeah, appreciate your help.’ Deano shoved his books into his backpack and hoisted it onto his back, ‘Come on, Scarlet.’

I ran after him as he shot off.

‘Where are you - ?’ I tugged at his sleeve.

‘It’s in my shoe.’ he hissed.

‘What?’

‘My *shoe*? I put it in my shoe.’ When we’d created a safe distance between us and the warden, Deano slowed down and breathed a sigh of relief. ‘I put it in there before we left, I forgot.’

‘Oh, jesus christ. So that was all for nothing?’

‘It wasn’t my fault he showed up!’

‘You idiot.’

He stifled a laugh and nodded towards the Student’s Union across the road.

‘Come on, let’s have a line.’

Chapter 5

Deep, hammering thumps vibrated the walls of the shabby, abandoned building. Climbing the concrete steps, we made our way to the sixth floor shrouded in darkness, only the muffled thumps of music as our guide. We’d arrived fashionably late by most standards, but at Johnny’s raves, half one in the morning was usually when things really kicked off. It was only our second time, but they had become somewhat of a hallmark on Belfast’s underground music scene, and the only place you could party with like-minded souls until five o'clock and openly snort any substance as if it were as acceptable as drinking a beer. The atmosphere was uniquely devoid of typical club snobbery, the crowd an inviting, eclectic mix of alternative hipsters, indie guitar players, artists and kids who listened to way too much Acid House. The vibe was one of heady indulgence, as if we were an extended family who had just discovered our own secret cave.

'Why would they hold an illegal rave at the top of the tallest bloody building they could possibly find?' I grumbled as we reached the top and opened a heavy, graffiti-covered door to reveal a chasm of thumping bass and flashing, multicoloured strobe lights.

'To make us earn it,' Deano grunted over the noise, wiping sweat off his brow.

Turns out we reaped the rewards of our labour. As soon as we'd been stamped and nodded in by the large, bearded man on the door known only as Jim, we headed straight to the smoking area. When I say smoking area what I really mean is a designated corner of the huge floor beside a large window, sectioned off by tie-dye drapes. I pushed through the bodies and peered around the growing crowd as I found us an old wooden cabinet to sit on. It wasn't packed yet, but there was a steady flow of people gathering, all saying their hello's or cocooning each other in bear hugs. I recognised a couple of faces, but there was only one person I actually wanted to see.

'He'll be here soon,' Lauryn yelled into my left ear.

Why did she have to be so bloody tuned in to my thoughts?

'Who?' I tried, and failed, to sound indifferent.

'You know who,' she laughed.

'I need a flat surface.'

'What?'

To rack up.'

'Oh.'

She jumped off the cabinet and I felt around in my pocket for the tiny plastic bag. I'd bought two grams of mephadrone off Deano, courtesy of my last student loan payment, seeing as the coke had run out. It was much cheaper than charlie, but burned your nose inside out and tends to make you edgy as hell if you go over your limit. Not to mention the terrifically horrendous piss smell that stuck to your clothes and sweated out of your pores for days. It was still hard to believe that just two years ago this stuff was legally bought in numerous alternative music and clothing stores in town. It was rumoured that a friend of Enya's had had a stroke after taking some, but these are the risks you take when you ply yourself with plant food. It was most likely an exaggerated story spread by scare-mongers. Stories like that evaporate from memory after a few lines. Once that dull void was filled, soothed and numbed sufficiently, fear was lost and invincibility took its place.

I felt my legs tingle and my heart start to race within minutes. I just wanted to move, and talk. Christ, I really needed to talk. About anything. I needed to absorb information, to learn everything about everyone. I struck up conversation with the guy beside us, eyes wide and continually tapping out a rhythm with my fingers on the cabinet. It wasn't long before I offered him a key. The urge to involve all those around me in my racing high had already kicked in, but I knew I'd have to go careful or I'd end up with nothing left.

'Isn't it weird that Jamie used to go out with Luke's sister?' Lauryn yelled.

I'd been trying to put it out of my mind, it just made me uncomfortable.

'Yeah, he didn't really say much. Just that he and Luke didn't get on.' I shouted back, my eyes flickering around the room and over each new face that appeared.

'Are you worried that she's prettier than you?'

'Lauryn!'

'Well obviously she isn't,' she babbled, 'But that's the first thing I'd think about.'

'Well now I *am* thinking about it.'

Except I'd already investigated and couldn't find her on any social networking site. I pulled my phone out of my bag and bought Jamie's Facebook page up on the screen. He still hadn't accepted my friend request, but he'd probably been too busy. I still had access to some of his photos and began flicking though them.

'Oh my God!' I screeched suddenly, 'Look.'

I showed Lauryn the screen. It was a photo of Luke with Jamie, holding pints, Jamie's arm around Luke's shoulder as if they were the best of friends.

'It must have been taken ages ago.' Lauryn said as she leaned in to inspect it closely.

'Hmm.'

One of the worst things about Belfast is how small it is. Circles of friends overlapped you seemed to have a mutual friend with everyone you met. Luke had mentioned Amber's name a few times, said she lived in the country now or something, but nothing of importance beside from that. There wasn't much time for further investigation right now anyway, despite the burning curiosity.

After chain-smoking four cigarettes I headed to the grotty toilet to have a private line to myself. I curled my lip in disgust at the putrid stench and questionable puddles on the broken-tiled floor. Where was Jamie? It was almost 2.30am. Wiping the cistern as best as I could, I took out a fiver and crushed the meph evenly.

'Fuck!'

I grimaced and cursed, sniffing as quickly as possible so as to endure minimal pain. Like ripping off a band aid. It still felt like someone had punched me in the nose and then pepper-sprayed my brain. I loved it, in a masochistic kind of way. My eyes watered and I looked around for some clean tissue. Some idiot was knocking on the door.

'In a minute!' I yelled.

The knocking continued. I managed to tear off the remains of a seemingly clean piece of tissue from the holder and dabbed my eyes, still shuddering at the rancid drip down the back of my throat.

'Alright!' I shrieked as I yanked open the door, 'Jesus, give me a

-'

It was his piercing eyes I saw first, and my words caught in my throat. Looking clean cut in a crisp white shirt, his skin swarthy and that curious half-smile, I tried not to sigh out loud at how ridiculously gorgeous he looked.

'Hello missus.'

'Oh, hey, Jamie.' I said,' Sorry.' I felt the blood rush to my cheeks.

'You look nice,' he smiled, 'although you've got something...'

He reached out and wiped under my right eye.

'Shit, yeah, it's the drone.' I clumsily waved his hand away, 'Want some?'

He pushed his way into the toilet and closed the door.

'Since when did you start on the miaow?' He watched me rack up another two lines.

'Since it was a lot cheaper than coke.'

'Makes sense.'

We hadn't really discussed the Luke situation, except for me confirming what a nut job he could be. But none of that really mattered right now. The questions I wanted to ask suddenly seemed irrelevant. I caught his gaze as he lifted his head from the cistern and rubbed his nose. His eyes made me still, calm.

'Come on,' he motioned.

Pushing through the now heaving mass of people jumping and fist-pumping to the music I edged towards Deano and Lauryn, the heavy scent of booze and sweat accumulating in what little air remained. Blinding lights danced furiously and distorted my vision as I scanned the area for Lauryn's bleached head, an illuminated buoy in the black sea of rave-goers.

Suddenly I felt a jolt of electricity through my arm as Jamie took my hand and pulled me back into the throbbing crowd. My heart hammered in my ears as he smiled, brazen as ever, and wrapped his arms firmly around my waist. I had been worried that our next meeting would be a disappointment, that maybe the pills had coloured my vision, and in reality he was nothing but an elaborate fabrication of my mind. But my second hit of Jamie was even more thrilling than the last. He had infiltrated my skin, spreading through my veins and enshrouding me in a heady opiate rush. With my arms wrapped around his neck, our bodies pressed together and moved in sync with the music as it gathered pace. I needed to move. My eyes closed as I felt every beat vibrate through my skin and my heart pulsating in tune. This was what it truly felt like to be alive. I submersed myself in the fervor of excitement and my fingers gripped his shoulder to pull him closer. Sweat began to drip down the small of my back and glistened on the figures around us that had faded and dulled into obscure shapes. It could easily have been just the two of us. His lips met the skin on my neck and I shivered. I couldn't seem to get close enough. I wanted to absorb him into my skin, my veins, to merge with every part of him.

Slipping his hand into the left pocket of my jeans, he enclosed his fingers around the little clear bag and my key for the flat. With one swift movement he dipped the key in and held it under my nose. I grimaced at the sharp burning sensation as meph shot up my nose and into my blood-flow at rapid speed. Jamie took his share and rubbed his finger over the metal to recover the remaining powder caught between the ridges. He looked at me intently, his face now inches away and I felt his warm breath on mine. I edged forward, but he reached up and put his finger to my lips. Tasting the bitter remnants of meph on my tongue, I grinned. He knew exactly which buttons to press. And just as I began to feel like I couldn't bare it any longer, he pulled away and motioned towards the smoking area. Did he know how much he was toying with me? I floated across the room, his hand in mine, and tried to shake the dizziness from my head.

My high didn't stop me from noticing Deano's poor efforts at disguising his apathy towards Jamie. A half-hearted wave with minimal eye-contact was about all he could muster. His was always quite reserved, but this was bordering on just plain rude. I glowered and opened my mouth to ask what his problem was. But then I saw Jamie envelope Lauryn in a bear hug as if they were old friends, and realised I was too giddy to react to any of Deano's bullshit. He'd get over it. There was very little that was going to pierce my inexplicable bubble of happiness.

The music raced in time with my heartbeat now. It seemed to gather speed with every line we sniffed. We danced relentlessly, the four of us, submersed in the buzzing frenzy of elated peoples intent only on maintaining their delirium. The air was sticky with sweat, and it wasn't long before we were lost in the crowd, bumping against strangers that with one pat on the back became friends. For the night, at least. I felt the eyes of almost every female, and a fair few males, hover on Jamie. I didn't blame them, he was magnetic. He exuded the charisma of someone that drew people in by his very nature, so inconveniently at ease with himself that he enticed without effort. His smooth features and devastatingly gorgeous smile beckoned an audience, but it was his energy that truly drew people in and he stood out like a sore thumb.

Shimmering strobes of rainbow colours flashed in the darkness, a black fog of energized bodies, smiles and screams. A watering hole for those who wanted to escape. It was our safe haven. The uneven walls vibrated with every drum beat and Jamie's face flashed intermittently through the blackness. A young scraggly-haired guy with bulging eyes painted elaborate swirls and patterns with luminous colours as high as the walls could go. It wasn't long before the yellows, greens and purple-pinks had seeped from them onto the faces of the participants of this great hypnotic gathering. A few volunteers took up paint brushes and soon the crowd was decorated with illuminated faces, flowers, spirals and stars. The accumulating vibration hummed in motion, and I was reminded of the close-up shots of atoms we were once shown back in school. Something about them moving faster and faster and bumping into each other rapidly to create heat. We were a microcosm of ecstatic particles, coagulating and intensifying. I briefly wondered how fast we could go, and just wished it would never end.

Jamie, at first an incongruous force-field of energy that dazzled the meager gray of his surroundings, now radiated and merged with the static atmosphere. It grew with every pump of the stereo, each resounding symphony, as faces flashed and glistened all around us. He coloured everything. I almost hated how in awe of him I was.

Jerking me violently out of my haze, Lauryn's urgent tugging on my elbow caused me to whip round and nearly lose my footing. Her eyes wide, she mouthed something I couldn't make out and her words were lost in the music. I shook my head in confusion.

She began fumbling around for her mobile, before thrusting the screen in my face as my eyes focused on the text message.

> Is that Jamie with Scarlet? I'll warn you, Luke is on his way. He won't be happy with that little prick.

It was from Luke's friend, Gary. Confused, I looked at Lauryn, who nodded behind me. Slouched against the wall was Gary, his lizard-like slits for eyes observing us from the shadows. He slugged from his beer, his eyes never moving from our direction. I eyed him back angrily.

'What?' I asked defiantly.

But no one heard a thing above the thumping noise. I broke my glare only to look around for Jamie. Searching the thick crowd, I frowned. He'd been right beside me a few moments ago. Bewildered, I turned around, but Gary had disappeared, too. Deano, sensing tension, raised his eyebrows quizzically.

Abruptly, Lauryn jumped like a scared cat and pulled out her vibrating phone. Her brow wrinkled.

'What is it?' I yelled in her ear.

She screamed something unintelligible at me.

'What?'

She leaned closer.

'Luke's here!'

Oh, fuck. Although I didn't exactly know why he and Jamie had such an issue with each other, I sensed I'd be the last person Luke wanted to see him with. Without waiting to hear any more, I sprinted off in search of Jamie. Any moment I expected to come face to face with Luke, like a guilty prisoner. Surveying the area, and with no sign of him, I made for the exit. There was no way I was going to risk Luke popping up in front of me like an unwelcome jack-in-a-box. My chest wheezed as I rattled down the stairs. They seemed to go on forever, and unwelcome exercise combined with copious amounts of stimulants did not make for comfortable breathing. After about a thousand years, I reached the bottom and pushed open the heavy fire exit door. The alleyway was black and cold, and spits of rain began to sting my cheeks. I took a right, towards the city center. There would be taxis there. But where the hell was Jamie? Cat-like, I slunk through the blackness before breaking into a jog that made the icy air rip at my throat. I slowed as I reached the main road of closed shops and cafes and randomly thought of what a shit state my hair must have been in. At that moment an arm gripped my elbow and yanked me into the nearest shop front. I clattered against the metal shutters and my heart almost launched out of my mouth.

'Jesus fucking Christ, what the - !'

'Shh!' Jamie's forehead glistened with rain and sweat. I detected the hint of a smirk on his face, my lack of refinement obviously amusing to him.

'Well I'm glad you think it's funny -'

He stiffened and beckoned me to be silent. The muffled sound of male voices began to echo in the alley. Then one, unmistakable, deep tone.

'I saw him go down there.' Luke definitely didn't sound

impressed.

Without hesitation, we were off again, heading down the cobbled road and onto the high street. Buildings whizzed by and clusters of clubbers screeched after us as we shoved past them. My body thumped and fizzled with adrenaline and my legs seemed to spiral off ahead of me, faster than I thought they were able to go.

'Down here.'

Jamie veered off down a side street leading to a dark car park where we skidded to a halt. I began giggling hysterically in between gasping for breath as we looked around for further escape. I took a moment to lean heavily against the concrete wall. Jamie was much fitter than me. He looked my way and began to snicker, running his hands through his damp hair. I laughed as he slipped his hand in mine and lead me across the car park and onto another dimly lit street. The flash of headlights blurred my vision as a black taxi crawled round the corner.

'Quick, taxi!' I yelled, tugging Jamie's soaking wet t-shirt.

The driver cursed and shook his head as we clambered on to the back seat. Jamie heaved the heavy door shut just as three shadows raced round the corner and shouted after us. I could just make out Gary's skinny frame behind two broader figures, which I presumed were Luke and another of his beefy tag-along mates. I waved out the back window, their bodies blurring and fading into nothing as rain streamed down the glass and washed them away completely.

I looked at Jamie and we both erupted into hysterics. Throwing my head back onto the seat, I gulped for air, shaking with laughter and adrenaline. I closed my eyes and felt my rain-soaked clothes clinging to my skin, but I didn't care. Jamie's hand was on my knee, and when he slid it down my inner leg I tingled all over. Sitting up, his face was already against mine and he pulled me closer, brushing my cheek with his lips.

'Take me home.' I whispered.

In a dizzy whirlwind we were kissing and laughing and throwing our coins at the taxi driver. Falling down the hall way to my room, the door slammed behind us and suddenly it was quiet. For once I was nervous in the best kind of way. Jamie pushed me onto the bed and tangled his fingers in mine, placing them above my head. I briefly caught his eyes burning into mine before he kissed my neck and sent shudders down my spine. He pulled away my clothes, his hands running down my body as I closed my eyes and soaked up every last moment. I gripped his waist with my thighs, pulling him as close as possible. I wanted our bodies to merge, to absorb every last part of him until we were a single being. I'd never wanted somebody so much, in every way, that it was never enough. The warmth of his skin against mine fueled my thirst, and I dragged my fingernails down his back. I tried to pull his hips closer to mine, and he held his hand around my face and neck. He would be the one to decide when, he had complete control. My lips were close to his again and I gasped as he pushed me down. I knew my eyes betrayed me, revealing my addiction. But I didn't care. He ran his fingers down my side, slowly brushing each curve, damp with sweat. I almost screamed in frustration. He had me exactly where he wanted.

And in one movement, he gripped my legs and his face came down to meet mine. I gave in completely, and so did he. Dizzy, beautiful and higher than I'd ever been before.

CHAPTER 6

It was that squalid time of morning where you just felt grubbier by the minute. A few hours after Jamie had slipped off to work that night I'd found myself restless again and had ended up at Enya and Cian's house. If I wasn't with him, I was thinking about him. And truthfully I just wanted to stay occupied until I could see him again. The tingling glow from the memory of our night together was starting to wear off so I sought out other means of staying high. I'd easily found the party, around fifteen people at Enya's place who had been on the go for two days since the rave, and managed to blag a few lines of charlie to keep me going. I wasn't certain how many days it had been, but I was pretty sure I was close to my five-day-party target that we'd talked about as part of our summer 'project'. But now the sun's judgmental rays penetrated the room to alert us to the day time, the hours where the rest of the world went to work and did normal things. I hated the light. It screamed that the night was over and it was time to come down. Lauryn had gone home to sleep hours ago, but Deano had turned up around the same time as me and so far was still standing. People had started to filter off and now only about eight remained. I wasn't ready to quit.

I peered around the kitchen, surveying each face to see who would fade and who would stay. I fiddled anxiously with the tap, filling the glass with water, pouring it out, then filling it again. God, my mouth was dry. I'd drank gallons of water but it still felt like a desert. And that ominous grey weight of depression and anxiety had begun to descend on my shoulders. I needed to sort this, and quick. What was required at that stage was the maintenance of the high, keeping it topped up enough to banish any signs of reality. If you managed to do that, you were set. It was a fine art...it was survival.

There were people sitting at the table on my left, cluttered with fag butts, filters and empty baggies, and a few others in a group on the floor to my right. I eyed the table crew, one thirty-something man with a guitar and three girls, including Enya. One of the girls could possibly make the cut, I could tell by the way she was talking at a hundred miles an hour, but Enya looked exhausted. Usually she ended up taking Valium and let us carry on downstairs while she went to bed. To my right, two guys in their late twenties, bickering over something political, looked like they might be in it for the long haul. But I couldn't be sure. A girl of about nineteen swayed slowly back and forth beside me, eyes staring into space. Guaranteed to quit within the next hour. Only the most dedicated wreck-heads would make the final cut. I wandered aimlessly into the living room to try and scope out Deano among the bodies standing, sitting, laying in every corner before approaching a girl with mad, curly locks of faded purple hair. Her name might have been Ellie, I couldn't remember.

'Hey. Yeah...hi. Are you guys starting to leave now or is anyone staying?'

'Ahh...yeah.' She nods vaguely, her eyes wide and darting around the room, 'I'm gonna stay for a while, I'll just leave whenever my friends decide to go home.'

She motioned to a small group laughing manically in the corner beside the portable heater.

'Glad someone else isn't ready to bail. This light is freaking me out, I wish it was night time again.' I said absent-mindedly.

'God, I know,' she waved towards the window. 'Someone shut the curtains!'

'Shut the curtains and keep 'er lit!' Cian had overheard us and raised his arm to his audience. He turned up the volume full whack on the iPod player and rocked his head of wild, ash-blonde locks back and forth. I grinned at him and the girl handed me a sniff of coke from her key before grabbing my hand. Soon we were jumping and wiggling to the frenzied techno beats once again. I spotted Deano on the sofa and waved at him. He lifted his beer and gave me a thumbs up. Once again I was ascending to where I needed to be.

After about twenty minutes of ridiculous dancing I collapsed in between Deano and his friend Anthony on the sofa. I laid my head back, gasping for breath as I heard my heart pumping wildly in my ears.

'Nice moves.' Deano said, sipping from his can.

'Thanks.' I knew he was taking the mick.

'Are you going to be ready to go soon?' he asked.

'Nope.'

'You're a fiend.'

'You're a fader.'

He rolled his eyes at me.

'Any coke left?' I ask hopefully.

'A little. Here,' he rummaged in his jacket front pocket. 'We'll go halves on whatever's left.'

'I think I've got some change left, I'll pay for a line.' I offered, sitting up. But Deano waved his hand dismissively.

'Put your money away, it's fine.'

'Thanks,' I said gratefully. 'You're so generous.' I lay my head on his shoulder.

'So you meant it when you said you were going to party hard this summer.' he observed as he carefully emptied the remains of the bag onto a DVD case. He pushed and chopped it around with his bank card like pieces of garlic until he'd formed two even lines and passed me the case.

'Yep, it's going to be an epic summer.'

I sniffed deeply, the bitterly potent chemicals burning right through to my brain. Within seconds the back of my neck tingled with the rush and I started jabbering faster than a Duracell bunny. Fuck, it was quality stuff.

'I've figured out that without any responsibilities, I can do all this without feeling bad about it. If you let go of the guilt and the pressure of being normal, you can just have all the craic. Don't know why I didn't think of it before. At the end of the day, I may not have a degree or a nice car, but at least I can say I've had a bloody good time.'

'Or you've just cracked and accepted less than you deserve or actually want.'

'What is that supposed to mean?' I demanded in irritation, 'Life's too short. It should always be like this.'

'What are you going to do, then?' Deano asked, 'Genuinely. I'm curious.'

'When?'

'In September, when the summer's over.'

'I'm going to become a mermaid.'

'Can't you just be serious for once?' he huffed.

'You're always serious.'

Anthony had been chuckling to himself beside us as he listened to our mindless bickering. I did know how to wind Deano up and we often clashed, but we'd never stay mad at each other for long.

'I recently read a book about mythological sea creatures.' Anthony announced.

'As one does.' I raised an eyebrow as he passed me the ends of a cigarette.

'There's actually some evidence to suggest mermaids do exist.' he told Deano seriously.

'Oh, for Christ's sake, don't encourage her.' Deano sighed.

'Really?' I chattered to anyone that would listen, 'I get bored of reading quite quickly. Mainly because I start one book and then three more at the same time. Once I get to a boring bit I just switch. So I sort of don't bother anymore.'

My jaw had started to ache from clenching it, and I could hear myself talking super fast yet couldn't slow down.

'You didn't answer my question.' Deano said flatly.

'What?'

'What are you going to do?'

I was sort of sick of being asked those questions. The more pressure I got, the more I wanted to just abandon society altogether. Maybe Jamie and I could go live on an island somewhere with mountains of coke and no one around to judge us.

'What are *you* going to do?' I shot back at him.

'Me? Well, I'll finish my course and then probably get a job.'

'Doing what?' I persisted.

'Wait, this is about you, not me.'

'Well I'm asking you now.'

'It doesn't matter, I'll have some options when I finish my degree.'

'But you don't have a plan.' I said bluntly.

Deano shook his head in exasperation and reached for another beer. He hated being wrong. Truth was, he was one of those people with a huge wealth of knowledge yet I doubt he'd ever do anything with it. If I had even half of his intellectual abilities I'd be more than happy. People are always banging on about utilising your skills. Maybe that's why he didn't. He remained somewhat stagnant, just like those geeky gaming figurines he collected of all his favourite characters. He bloody loved them, and spent hours online trying to find limited edition dragons and hobbits or whatever they were. He rearranged them sometimes but other than that they just sat there, frozen. Boring. I lived according to my own rules. And right now, it was hard to think of anything I wanted other than to be with Jamie and staying like this forever. Living on our own terms and being truly free...surely that was the most wonderful legacy anyone could leave.

The minor shift in energy, however, had started to bring me down. And this time there was no coke left to lift me up again. That was the thing about cocaine, there was never enough. As the last of it wore off, I began to feel heavy and the sound of people's chattering became irritating. I'd just begun to begrudgingly accept defeat when the doorbell rang and everyone looked up expectantly. More people meant the possibility of more drugs. Cian darted towards the door and muffled voices sounded on the other side. I heard the clanking of bottles and rustling carrier bags as Cian swung the door open and Jamie and two other guys I didn't recognise piled into the room. My stomach twirled and suddenly my mood soared. They chatted between themselves for a moment before Jamie spotted me and pulled a face playfully, beckoning me over.

'Hi,' I embraced him apprehensively in a hug. Seeing him for the first time since the night of the rave made me nervous. 'How are you?'

'I'm good,' he murmured. 'You?'

'Great,' I grinned contentedly, 'Have you just finished work?'

'Um, yeah. Long day.' Every time I caught his gaze my heart

jumped, 'Is there any coke around?'

'No, sorry. I've ran out of cash. But I think Anthony has some to sell.'

'Damn.' He looked disappointed, 'No cash on me.'

I saw his expression and suddenly feared he might leave again.

'Hang on.' I said.

I went over to the purple-haired girl again but hesitated. It was unlikely she's spare me any, and I didn't know her well enough to strap some of her. Instead, I scooted over to Deano and looked at him anxiously.

'Deano. You know the way I'm like one of your best friends?' I said innocently.

'Oh God, what do you want?' he sighed.

'Could I possibly borrow some cash off you until next week? I'll give you an extra tenner for interest.'

'What do you want it for?'

'Um, I need to get another gram... He raised his eyes, 'But! It's just to last me the week. You know I always pay you back.' I pleaded.

I knew he wouldn't give it to me if he thought it was for Jamie, too. He paused, shaking his head and scratching at his beard.

'Oh, fine. But you're doing the washing up all week. And you'll promise to cut down after this'

'Deal.'

'I'll just get one off Anthony and put it on my bill, I don't have the cash on me.'

'Thank you,' I squeaked excitedly. He mumbled something in Anthony's ear and handed me the bag as I jumped up and skipped over to Jamie.

'Sorted.' I beamed, holding up the bag.

'No way!' That gorgeous smile lit up his face and I felt like I'd just won the lottery, 'You're amazing.'

He grabbed me by the waist and planted a kiss on my lips. I giggled happily like a school girl.

'Not just a pretty face,' I teased.

'Definitely not. Hey,' he leaned towards me and lowered his voice, 'let's go do this in the bathroom so we don't have to hand out free lines to any of these scroungers.'

I nodded and followed him as we slipped out of the living room and up the stairs. The bathroom was right at the top and Jamie ushered me in and locked the door behind us. Immediately he turned to me and pulled my body against his, kissing me passionately. I sank into his arms and felt the hairs on the back of my neck stand on end. My hands pressed against his chest as our kisses gradually became lighter.

'I was about to have a pretty bad come down before you came.' I said quietly.

He smiled and pushed a tendril of hair behind my ear, his

beautifully deep blue eyes slowly surveying mine.

'Wanna get high?'

'Obviously.' I grinned as he let go of me and leaned over the cistern to lay out some lines,

'I hate this time of day, when you've been out all night. It's so...quiet. And sad. Like the rest of the world is this big, foreign place.'

'Well in that case, let's just power through till it's night time again.' he said as he handed the rolled up note to me.

And it really was that simple. If I could guarantee staying high for the day, nothing else was of any real relevance.

As I bent over he sat down on the lid of the toilet. I realised how filthy Enya had let her bathroom get, and imagined how unhygienic it must be to be sniffing off any form of surface in here. You couldn't really think like that though, not if you wanted a line that badly. It was just a matter of priorities.

'Does nothing ever scare you then?' I asked curiously.

'I don't get scared. I'm invincible.'

He looked at me with a mischievous glint in his eyes as I sat down on his lap.

'There must be something.'

I tapped him playfully on the nose and then wrapped my arms around his neck.

'Nope.' he said definitively. I cocked my head to the side and looked at him, unconvinced. He looked down thoughtfully, 'Well, I hate losing control. I'm scared shitless of being trapped, or of not being in charge of everything around me,' I was quiet for a moment, 'I've never told anyone that.' he said eventually as he looked up and smiled.

I kissed him gently on the forehead. I'd somewhat softened that dense exterior of his and I ached to be closer to him. But just as quickly as he'd opened up, he changed the subject.

'I like this,' he said, toying with the buttons on my pale yellow summer dress.

'This?' I said, surprised, 'It's old.'

He pulled me closer and pressed his lips against my neck.

'I'd like it better off you, though.' he whispered and my insides shivered.

'We can't,' I said, standing up, 'not here.'

'Why not?' He stood up and put his hands around my waist again, bringing his face close to mine. I was immediately entranced.

'Because...' I started but he caught me in a kiss. I gave in and my arms instinctively went up to clasp his face, pressing myself against him. Soon our kisses became more urgent.

'Nope...' I pulled away suddenly. I could barely resist him but I wanted to know more. He was so difficult to read, I might not get this chance again for ages and I wanted to be tied to him in every way I could.

'What's wrong?' he pulled away, bemused, as I rested my hands on his shoulders.

'Where do you live?' I looked at him curiously.

'What...why?' he laughed.

'Just wondering,' I shrugged, 'With friends?'

'Sometimes.'

'With your parents?'

'Nope.'

'Where did you grow up?' He just smiled that infuriatingly sexy way he always did. I studied his face, the firm line of his jaw, those soft lips I couldn't stop kissing. 'Stop being so mysterious. It's cliched.'

He winked at me and I rolled my eyes, trying my hardest to be serious. But I couldn't even get annoyed with him. All he had to do was touch me and I was completely his once again. After a few minutes I realised we were swaying back and forth.

'What are you doing?' I said quietly.

'Dancing,' he said tenderly, taking my hand and slowly twirling me around.

'Charmer,' I said as my fingers became entwined with his.

I leaned in and rested my head on his shoulder, as if we'd done it a hundred times before. It always felt natural, we just fit. He began to kiss my neck delicately again, his hand ran smoothly up my left side then round to the buttons at the front of my dress. As his kisses became firmer against my skin I didn't stop him as he undid them one at a time before letting my dress fall to the floor. I cradled the back of his head and returned his kisses by running my tongue softly over his earlobe. Just as his fingertips traced the outline of my underwear, a tremendous banging made us jump apart

'Hey!' Cian yelled outside the bathroom door, 'You in there?'

'What is it?' Jamie called back irritably.

'You've gotta go,' his voice lowered slightly, 'Gary's here, Luke's mate. He's saying they've been looking for you and that you're in for a kicking. You need to bounce before he sees you, I don't want any trouble in my house. The neighbours hate me as it is.'

'Fuck.' Jamie muttered as I hurriedly pulled my dress up and began buttoning it.

'He won't do anything, he's all talk.' I babbled.

'I gotta go.' he gave me a quick kiss and unlocked the door, darting down the stairs after Cian.

'Wait, where are you - ?' I shouted after him.

'I'll text you.' he called over his shoulder as the front door banged shut.

I stood there for a few minutes with my dress half buttoned, confused. Why was he so worried? Luke could be intimidating, I'd admit, but he couldn't run from him forever. I sighed and leaned against the sink. He'd come and gone like a whirlwind, and I could still feel the tingle on my skin where his lips had brushed my shoulder. Again, I was left wanting more. And then something occurred to me. I went to the cistern, tracing my hands over the cold porcelain, but it was gone. He'd taken the coke with him, which left me with nothing to soften my come-down. I sank to the floor, my head resting in my hands. Those volatile ups and downs had left me dizzy and disorientated, and I finally admitted defeat. I stood up to go and tell Deano I was ready to leave, hoping that with any luck I might just sleep through till the next time.

Chapter 7

It was especially humid, even for July. Summer always brought Johnny and his team the opportunity to cash in on outdoor events. They had recently launched a series of semi-legal garden raves in a cluster of woodland, rose gardens and rolling lawns stretching over ten acres of land just outside the city. A deal had been forged with the park owner whereby, in return for receiving a third of the entrance fees, he agreed to host a mini-festival in a quiet sect of the area, far enough into the woods so as not to attract any police attention. I'd begun to think the whole thing was a hoax as Deano, Lauryn and I clambered through pitch black wooded pathways, the rich scent of bark filling my nostrils. It was the only thing that reassured me of our whereabouts and that we hadn't fallen into some dark void. Lauryn clutched my hand as I used the other to shine my phone light on the barely-trodden ground before us. It was just past midnight, but the canopy of trees shut out the moonlight. We cursed our way through the darkness, bumbling and bashing into each other like clowns. It briefly occurred to me that we always seemed to be clambering around weird places in search of a party.

Eventually, a dimly lit track emerged leading us to a man guarding a black range rover. I looked at him uncertainly as I handed over the ten pound fee, but he motioned us in enthusiastically. Beyond the neighboring hedgerow, the three of us gasped as we revealed a wonderland of carved wooden seats, roaring camp fires and a little stone pathway, lit by a million fairy lights.

'Whoa.' Deano nodded, impressed.

'Look at the trees!' I cried. Scarfs in a multitude of colours were wrapped carefully around the trunks, as if the organisers had not wanted the foliage to be left out. At the far end of the garden a small stage had been formed, gigantic speakers marking each side and the delicate strums of guitar seeping from their depths. Guests were now scattered across the grass, using stretches of tarpaulin to create little island seats. We gawped at our surroundings and moved to a central space near the stage. We found ourselves among a group of about seven, including Molly, a singer with hauntingly beautiful vocals who would no doubt be performing later. Enya was also there with Oliver, a regular who was never seen without his guitar.

'Scarlet, Lauryn...this is Isaac.' Molly introduced us to a broad man with shiny black eyes and an even brighter smile. 'He's moved over here from Nigeria.'

'Hi,' I smiled, waggling my fingers at him. 'Good to have you here.'

It wasn't uncommon for immigrants to find their way into our group, not simply for our warmth and diversity, but also because this free-floating existence was a strange source of comfort and security for all of us. We chatted like excitable birds, swigging from our wine bottles as the music played gently around is. But a part of me couldn't quite fully relax. I almost hated how much Jamie had me so firmly in his grip, hated and loved it all at the same time. How fucked up was that? And then I caught a glimpse of him in the small crowd to the left of the stage and my heart jumped. Ruffling my hair as discreetly as possible and attempting to tame the wild ends, I started to rejoin the others in conversation, only slightly peeved at myself for being such a stereotypical girl. I hadn't seen him since the house party over a week ago and had made do with a handful of texts and phone calls.

'So, is it good?' Lauryn's voice came from over my left shoulder.

'Is what good?'

'The sexy-time with Jamie.'

I turned round to face her.

'A lady never tells.' I announced coyly, turning up my nose and taking a puff on my cigarette.

'You always tell.' she said flatly.

'No I d- ' I dropped my cigarette and the sophisticated, Audrey Hepburn-esque act was ruined. Lauryn looked at me, one eyebrow raised.

'Ok, I do.'

She wiggled closer, ears poised for information and gory details. I paused, then leaned in and whispered, 'Well, we've only done it once but...It was amazing.'

She almost screeched with glee, 'That's fantastic!'

'No, it's not.' I replied bluntly.

'What...why?' she frowned, puzzled.

'Because it means I'm in big trouble. It means I've given him what all men want on a biological level and he could very well just run off and leave now. And I'll just be sitting here...used, ruined and...and...a spinster.'

'A spinster?'

'Yes. Once you've had the best sex ever, any proceeding encounters will pale in comparison. So if he leaves me I'll end up alone with lots of pet gerbils, yearning after my lost youth. And the worst part? He knows it. He knows what he's done and he knows that I know too.'

There was a brief silence. Then Lauryn burst into fits of laughter, hitting me with a barrage of spittle in the process.

'You're so dramatic!'

'No, I'm not. See? He hasn't even come over yet. Oh God, it's happening. I really am ruined.' I groaned.

Lauryn rolled her eyes and threw a cigarette at me. I was right, though, he hadn't come over yet. He *must* have seen me. I'd strategically placed myself, and my shiny turquoise bomber jacket, right in the epicenter of the party. As I began hopelessly catastrophising, I fumbled restlessly with my phone, reading the same Facebook newsfeed posts over and over until I almost flung it into the prickly rose bushes. By the time the DJ had started his set, I had had enough.

'Lauryn, I'm really not in the mood. I think I'll - '

'Alright madam.' I felt his hands around my waist. He twisted me round and pulled me to him.

'Oh...hello.' I mumbled.

Then I saw his intensely penetrating eyes and I melted. Right when I thought I'd figured him out, he surprised me. I wrapped my arms around his firm waist as he kissed me softly on the forehead.

'I missed you.' I blurted out before I had time to think. He smiled, the hypnotic glint that pulled me in over and over.

'I missed you, too.'

That made my insides go all squidgy and warm.

'Fancy a drink?' I motioned to our seated area, keen to distract him from my obvious vulnerability. He squeezed between me and Lauryn, greeting her with a kiss on the cheek that made her giggle. The fact that he charmed her made me happy. I desperately wanted them all to like him, especially Deano, who never spoke to him directly. Instead, he responded generally to the group whenever Jamie asked a question. I pushed it out of my mind, there was no point in letting it bother me.

'Enya has trips,' Deano said as he looked at me, obviously pondering the thought.

'As in LSD?' I asked.

'Kind of. Synthetic psilocybin. It's in magic mushrooms.'

'*Proper* psilocybin.'

'Yes, *proper.*'

'Well I guess we could tick it off the list.' I said to Lauryn excitedly.

I'd never taken trips before. I was wary, but the idea of untouched ground had already begun to fester, and before I'd even opened my mouth to reply I knew what the answer would be.

'Well if we're all going to...' I looked around at the others.

'Could be fun, especially out here.' Deano said.

Molly's husky tones breezed through the air, rich and delicate like the yellow roses. Her voice tickled and enticed my curiosity, and I turned to watch her on the stage. Soft lighting illuminated the left side of her face as she held the mic stand close like it was a precious stone, and whisps of deep auburn hair danced gracefully around her head. Once again that burning urge to push the boundaries, to explore and to thrill my mind, returned. I took a swig of white wine.

'Let's do it.' I faced Jamie, 'It's going to be awesome.'

He could see it in my face. I knew the allure of the unknown thrilled him too.

'I'm up for it.' he agreed.

Deano instantly disappeared and returned minutes later holding a handful of red and blue capsules containing a minuscule amount of white powder.

‘Fiver each.’ he waved it in the air and nodded towards us.

‘Cheap as chips.’ I said, surprised.

‘And better than any chips you’ll ever have.’ he winked.

It was half an hour before things started to get weird. I’d spent a while chain-smoking and talking to Isaac about global warming, and had whined impatiently to Deano that nothing was happening. Oisin had begun to strum his guitar, the chords mingling unsettlingly with the trance anthems now pulsating from the decks. I leaned against Jamie and inhaled his intoxicating scent. A silent buzz fizzled and grew across the garden. People were beginning to get drunk, or coming up on whatever drugs they were on. Lauryn sat cross-legged opposite me, chittering away to Deano. I observed the scene as if it were a dress rehearsal for its debut night at the theatre, we were all waiting for the big show. I frowned. Suddenly I began to feel detached, lingering between the garden grasses and some obscure dissociative state. Something was pulling me in a foreign direction, and I was reluctant to let go. I shifted uncomfortably and began anxiously pulling at my sleeve, trying to focus on my breathing. If I could just stay calm, maybe it would pass. I looked around and studied everyone’s face, one at a time. No one else seemed to be concerned. Fuck, I was going to lose my mind. What if I never came back from this?

Everyone’s brain activity had started to increase. Conversations became louder and overlapped, colours became more vivid and I was pretty sure everything was sliding. Complete sensory overload as new mental pathways collided, expanded and bashed into one another. Nope, I did not like this. Not one bit. I'd changed my mind, I wanted to be normal again.

'Deano' I called out.

He stopped mid-sentence as soon as he saw the look on my face, bewilderment and the hint of fear etched around my eyes.

'Relax,' he reached out and squeezed my knee. 'You're just crossing over to the other side. Don't fight it, or you'll freak out. Just go with it.'

Go with it. Go with *what*?

At that moment, Jamie stood up and motioned for me to follow him.

'Let's go for a walk.' he said.

'Probably a good idea.' Deano agreed.

I let him lead me down a skinny stone path, half-lit by flickering lanterns. We reached a small, leafy alcove where someone had attached a hammock from the over-stretched branches above. I gripped the edge of the material and lowered myself into it.

'It'll pass.' Jamie reassured, 'Just relax.'

I looked up and his expression seemed safe and comforting. That was until his skin started rippling like waves on the ocean. I turned away and, to my horror, the ground had started to move in the same way. Vibrating, shifting, in constant motion.

'I don't know what's happening.' I tried to explain, 'Nothing's how it's supposed to be.'

I knew it sounded daft out loud. I just wanted the ripples of anxiety deep in my stomach to stop, and for something to feel familiar.

'Lauryn.' I mumbled.

'What?' Jamie shifted uncertainly, his own trip had obviously started kicking in. His eyes had sort of zoned out.

'Can you get Lauryn?' I asked. He looked confused for a moment, then shook his head as if to clear a dusty cloud from around it.

'Oh, yeah. Okay. Hang on.'

He drifted off into the darkness, the trees swallowing him whole and leaving me swaying gently, listening to the babble of voices just meters away and the low hum of the bass. One, two. One, two. I swayed carefully and with concentration in time with the waves. One, two. Soft and regular, the sound of the tide lapping against the shore soothed and steadied me. I closed my eyes to hear it moving effortlessly, in and out. One, two. The ripples in my stomach were still alive, but I had joined them now. One, two. One, two. Wait a minute, I thought., There is no sea around here. Not for miles. What the -

Before I could figure it out another wave surged right through me. I practically launched out of the hammock and creased over like a rag doll, vomit spewing spectacularly from me like a river unleashed from a dam.

I felt Lauryn beside me, and realised she too was violently throwing up, a torrent of puke splashing onto the soil beneath us. The two of us groaned and heaved as, gradually, the splatters filtered down to weak trickles of bile and spit. We knelt there in silence for what seemed a lifetime, breathing heavily.

'So much better.' My voice was weak with relief.

'Definitely.' Lauryn gasped.

Knowing that someone else was feeling what can only be described as intensely messed up made me feel a bit better.

'Is it supposed to be like this?' I asked.

'Deano said to just give in to it and relax.'

'That's pretty hard to do when the ground is swirling around your feet,' I laughed and stood upright.

'He said nothing bad is going to happen, we just have to go with the flow and then we'll enjoy it,' she explained.

'Right,' I said, 'Enjoy the weirdness.'

'Enjoy the weirdness.' she nodded.

The waves had steadied and the uncertainty began to dissipate. Something was very different, but it no longer scared me. Like being whisked away and thrown on a train, blindfolded, the journey there was traumatic but once we arrived, there was nothing to fear. It surprised me how quickly things had changed. I straightened up, still trembling slightly, and pulled out tissues to clean myself up. Lauryn handed me a bottle of water and some minty gum. At least we were well equipped.

'Gross, at least Jamie didn't witness the epic vom session. He wouldn't have come near my face again.'

'He's too busy entertaining the others,' Lauryn said, 'I ran off to puke after laughing too much.'

'Isn't he freaking out? He didn't look too good either.'

'He seemed okay. I think they all got up to dance.' Lauryn fluffed her hair and checked herself for puke remnants.

'We should join them.' I linked my arm in hers.

I couldn't have physically or mentally handled dancing ten minute ago. I guess it all affected us differently.

'Yeah...the trees are starting to dance. This is most definitely a good thing.' she said absentmindedly, gazing in awe at the canopy of branches above.

I craned my neck back and inhaled a fresh gulp of air. I felt reborn. I'd made some almighty transition, and anything seemed possible. The fizz of magic lit up my fingertips and I felt a surge of power beneath my skin. It was as if I'd been given a blank canvas and an array of colours with which to paint an adventure of my choosing. I lifted my right hand and slowly waved it over the night sky, glittery trails following close behind each finger and decorating the spindly old arms of the oaks. The world had opened up in 3D and suddenly I was seeing everything from numerous angles, as if for the first time.

My mind was incredibly active, except now the thought loops were becoming enjoyable. I became lost in my head as I observed them peacefully.

'Well, this is sort of wonderful.' I breathed with satisfaction.

The hum of voices lured me towards the trail path. I had an urge to socialize, to engage with other human beings. I yanked Lauryn away from her magic trees and we scuttled back to the crowd. Jamie looked up as I plonked myself down.

'Feeling better?' he eyed me cautiously, as if expecting me to turn into the girl from The Exorcist at any moment.

'Much.' I smiled.

I had broken down a barrier in my own mind, letting my thoughts wander and overlap at their own will, my eyes see whatever unfolded around me. I let go of the fear that had engulfed me and jostled violently in my stomach with every passing minute, opening the gateway to a place of complete freedom and knowing.

'Ego-loss,' Deano announced, peering at me.

'Pardon?'

'That scary, strange experience you just had. And the process of giving in to it and letting go. That's the loss of the ego, the part of you that judges everything and tries to make sense of the world by labeling everything that's going on. You need to do lose that in order to have a good trip.' he explained.

'Well thanks for letting me know beforehand, asshole!' I exclaimed before laughing, 'Right after I've puked half my guts up.'

'You figured it out all by yourself.' he grinned, 'So did you.' he nodded to Lauryn. She looked at him, puzzled.

'Don't worry Lolly, he's talking crap.'

But I needn't have worried. She quickly became engrossed in the wisps of grass around her feet. I sort of understood what Deano was saying, though. Crossing the boundary between reality and trippy-land had been the difficult part. But once you're over the proverbial line, you know it was definitely worth it.

'They're wiggling like worms!' Lauryn snorted with laughter, fixated on the grass. 'Marching in time with the music.'

I glanced at Deano and Jamie, and we instantly burst into fits of giggles.

'Right, let's get her away from the green worm army,' Jamie held out his hand, 'Dance with me?'

We danced without inhibitions, the four of us, arms flailing, heads banging and laughing incessantly. I twirled Lauryn around and she grew butterfly wings, purple and gold and frail. Jamie lifted me up and swung me until the ground became the sky and faces turned into goblin heads. I don't know how long we carried on like that, but it seemed as though everyone else in the crowd was in the same parallel universe as we were, where time became obsolete. I clasped strangers in embraces and laughed as I told them they were all part of this magical goblin dance.

Eventually, we collapsed in a heap around one of the fires, now burning less ferociously but still throwing sparking embers in every direction. Kaleidoscopic patterns rippled through the flames and I could barely take my eyes off them. Jamie serenaded us with his impressions before describing every colourful detail of his Batman-themed hallucinations on the dancefloor. We fell about laughing like it was the funniest thing on earth until tears gathered in my eyes. I caught Lauryn by the shoulder just as she bent over and a flame almost caught her hair.

'Careful Lollipop, we nearly had you thrown back into the fires from whence you came.'

'Burn the witch!' Enya chorused.

'I am not a witch.' Lauryn pouted.

'I feel like a witch.' Deano mused to himself.

I squeezed Lauryn tight. I wanted her to know how much I needed her. I wanted everyone to know how much I appreciated them being here, but I think they already did. Damn, the human empathy buzz was strong. Then once again my mind was drawn to my magic fingertips. I pondered them for a moment and flung my hands haphazardly in every direction to see if I could make things spark into fire.

'What are you doing?' Deano looked at me, amused.

'Just honing my wizard skills.' I explained.

'You need to seriously check yourself.'

'We'll all need to check ourselves for about a month after this.' We both started to laugh again and I rested my chin on my palm. 'Do you ever think about the way people assume they're all human beings with different minds running around doing their own thing, when really we're all one big consciousness just separated into various forms?'

'Well, yes. That's one of the biggest lies we tend to live by, the illusion of separateness. We all evolved and expanded from the same molecules and are still essentially just that. It makes sense.'

'Sort of blows my mind. But trust you to intellectualise it.' I smiled. 'It's going to be majorly shit when this wears off.'

'That's the trouble.' he mumbled.

'Do you think there's a limit to how many amazing experiences you can have? Like, once you've reached a certain point you either become immune to everything or go completely nuts?'

'Maybe.' he lit a cigarette carefully and pondered the thought.

'I don't understand why everyone doesn't trip now and again, just to keep themselves right. Normal life just seems like an illusion now. So fake and bland.'

'Or we've lost the ability to find the beauty in reality. Although reality itself is subjective...' He raised an eyebrow. I could almost hear the mental cogs of his brain whirring in motion.

'There's nothing beautiful about reality.' I scoffed.

'But you're right,' Deano continued, bringing the fag to his lips and inhaling deeply. 'We're a youth culture of hedonists, Scarlet. And we'll drink, sniff, love and laugh ourselves into nothingness.'

'What a wonderful way to go.' I breathed contentedly.

I watched the flames licking the air for a moment, mesmerised by their hypnotic dance. Every particle of being vibrated in a constant movement. Us, the trees, the laughter. My mind seemed to have curled open like a flower in bloom and the best part was I knew everyone was experiencing the same. We were all in this vibrant, new reality together.

Jamie threw his head back and laughed at something Oliver said and I smiled to see him so happy. He drew the attention of everyone with his energy, teasing and playing, just being Jamie. I caught Enya's eyes on him and for a moment was instinctively jealous. I touched his hand, he curled his fingers around mine and I relaxed. He was with me and I could almost burst with pride as I watched him. I was his, and he'd brought me to life.

Deano was explaining the 'collective consciousness' to Oliver and my attention turned to their conversation as he quietly strummed his guitar. With every new piece of information I uncovered, it opened another psychological door to untrodden ground. I almost couldn't keep up with my thoughts but watched them in amazement as they flowed in directions they'd never gone before. I finally understood what all those mad hippies from the 60's had been talking about.

'We're all small, but essential, connected parts of a bigger picture. Psychedelics simply open your mind to that realisation.'

'It's pretty cool to feel so insignificant yet so essential at the same time.' I interjected.

'The dichotomy of creating and having been created. Ying and Yang.' Oliver nodded knowingly to himself and I almost laughed at how ridiculous we would sound to most people.

'This is pretty intense.' I said as I moved over and crouched beside Lauryn.

'I'm all...alive and stuff.' Lauryn took my hand in hers.

I smiled because I knew that feeling was hard to put into words.

'We're all in sync. It's lucky we have such a good bunch of people here.' I said.

'Like magnets.'

'Exactly.'

Trailing spirals danced on her small, pointed features like mini fireworks.

'So, I guess this means we're tripping.' she observed, swaying in time to Oliver's delicate guitar rifts.

'We've been tripping since 1am. I'd say we're in Stage 5 now.'

'What's Stage 5?' she asked, confused.

'The phase after the point where you realise you've been tripping for five hours,' I explained.

'And what about Stage 3?' she raised an eyebrow skeptically.

'The phase where you realise there are phases.'

'And after all that?'

'Phase 6. Where all phases become obsolete.'

I looked at her seriously for a moment but couldn't keep a straight face and burst into belly-aching laughter at the sight of her bemused expression.

'What a load of shit,' Deano laughed and shook his head.

Cian briefly looked up from his spot on the muddy ground before furrowing his brow and getting back to examining his fingers as if they were made of gold.

‘See,’ I nudged Lauryn, ‘he’s clearly still in Phase 3.’

We cackled as Oliver waved his hands in the air to silence the group before he spoke in his soft, calming tone.

‘I’ve thought of a song,’ he told us shyly. ‘I only have the two verses and a chorus but you’re welcome to sing along. It’s about tonight.’

We all fell silent as he began to play the strings and delicate strums filled the air around us. His voice flowed with ease as if he’d sung it a thousand times.

‘Beauty like I’ve never seen,

Purple, blue and white and green,

Do you know how you look tonight?

These are the reasons, these are the times we’re living for,

And if anyone asks, I don’t want for nothing more.

Go to the places you’ve never been,

See the things you’ve never seen,

Look at what we’ve made tonight.

These are the reasons, these are the times we're living for,

And if anyone asks, I don't want for nothing more,

These are the reasons, these are the times we're living for,

And if anyone asks, I don't want for nothing more.'

H sang and it was beautiful. It was even more beautiful when we cracked up laughing about how ludicrously hippy-ish we'd become in such a short space of time.

Jamie began to trail his hand slowly down my back and I felt the fibers of my skin ignite. I turned to him and once more an intense rush passed through me. Would I ever get tired of him?

'What do you think?' I said in his ear.

'About what?' he pushed a black tendril of hair behind my ear.

'Is this better than reality?'

He paused, his eyes now resting on mine.

'Every time.'

'I'll never forget this.'

My phone beeped and it felt like a sound from another planet. I reluctantly pulled away a looked at the screen.

> Where are you? I left you voice mails. Let me know you're alright. Mum x

I recoiled from the device as if it had an infectious plague. I did not want to be reminded of anything normal right now. I put it on silent and pushed reality into the depths of my jacket pocket.

Daylight had begun to spread across the park. People had sectioned off into fragmented groups, the melancholy air of morning gently winding everyone down.

'Do you want to go home?' I leaned in to whisper in Jamie's ear. I knew that flat grimness of day was on the horizon, but I didn't want to be there to witness it. I figured if Jamie and I kept running it wouldn't find us. He flashed a cheeky half-smile in agreement and we made our excuses. Lauryn and Deano were discussing moving on to an after-party nearby. As we reached the path leading to the main entrance where our taxi waited, I heard my name being called.

'Hey! Scarlet, wait.' Lauryn screeched to a halt as we turned around, breathless, with some piece of foliage stuck in her hair. She thrust her bag at me.

'I can't believe you're not coming.' she looked disappointed, 'But take this if you are. I can't bring my camcorder to the party, it's bound to get nicked.'

'Well just be safe.' I hoisted the bag over my shoulder, 'And make sure you stick with Deano.'

She was off again, waving wildly as she ran down the path to join the others. I didn't mention the twig in her hair. It added to the woodland-sprite look, and she probably wouldn't care anyway. For once, I didn't feel like I was missing out on a party. My mind and body were still buzzing, and spending time alone with Jamie was enough today. I didn't need much else.

I rested my head on his shoulder in the back of the taxi, letting the delicious flows of energy ripple through me. As we approached my street Jamie took out his wallet to pay the driver.

'Who's that?' I pointed to a photo inside it. A little girl of about two, dressed in blue with sandy curls around her face. She was smiling.

'My niece.' He said.

I never got to hear about his family. He didn't say anything else so I didn't ask. He leaned forward and handed a note to the drive. 'Cheers, mate.

I thought about asking again but decided against it.

We stumbled into the living room of my flat, the hallucinations now fleeting and difficult to grasp. I instantly made a cocoon on the floor with the sofa throw, on old blue blanket and some cushions. Nestled beside Jamie, we talked for hours, the sun steadily creeping towards noon, his fingers gently tickling my arm and shoulders.

'Are you worried about Luke?' I said suddenly. Jamie seemed to tense a little and I almost regretted opening my big mouth.

'Not worried, no. We shouldn't tell anyone we've been...hanging out, though.'

I wasn't sure what that meant. But I feared if I pressed him too much I'd lose him. Though, as exhilarating as it was hiding and sneaking around like teenagers, I yearned for something more solid. Eventually we would have to find a way to be open about it, or what was the point?

I shifted onto my side to look at him, my head resting on his outstretched arm. My eyes rested on the flop of hair over his forehead. He pushed it away yet somehow it always made its way back there. I traced the outline of his face with my finger, the strong jaw, the soft lips with that permanent hint of a smile. So much passed between us even when we said nothing. At first it made me nervous, how his eyes bore right through me. It was as if he could see me better than I could see myself. Now I welcomed it. It told me I could trust him, and I wanted to give him every part of me.

'Don't leave me.' It came out with more fear than I'd intended.

'Where do you think I'm going?' he murmured softly.

My hand rested on his neck now, gently stroking the bottom of his earlobe. Faint trails of colour still ebbed from my fingertips as they moved, and the texture and tones of his skin looked deep and intricate.

'I don't know. I just worry I'll lose you.'

He looked at me for a moment, and I was surprised to see a vulnerability in his eyes, as if maybe he too saw some kind of danger if this ended. He reached for my face, pulling me closely towards his. His lips rested against mine, barely touching. We lay like this for a while, absorbed in each other.

'I can't seem to get enough of you.' I breathed, still lingering over his lips. He responded with a firm kiss, clutching my head towards his. I realised he often didn't answer my questions in words. I saw in his eyes what he wanted to say, but often the message was clouded. He was holding something back, something precious that he didn't want to give away.

He kissed my nose, my mouth, my forehead. I closed my eyes and inhaled his scent. 'You're gorgeous.' he said as he took his hand from beneath his head and stroked from my neck down to my hip bones, teasing the sensitive part of my stomach above them.

Shivering, our breathing became heavier and he grabbed me round the waist in a firm grip.

'Come here,' he ordered, and pulled me on top of him. I leaned down to kiss him, feeling my body on fire and wanting more every second. I kissed him harder, his tongue pushing deep into my mouth. Then it was just happening, my body grinding desperately on his, his hands gripping my thighs. And I lost myself all over again.

Chapter 8

The comedowns were getting worse. When I wasn't doing coke I was thinking about ways to get it. When everybody else faded into sleep I sat in my bedroom and sniffed alone until that was all gone too. At that point my only option was to take a few sleeping tablets so I could stay unconscious for as long as was needed until I was re-energised enough to obtain more.

Jamie was MIA again. I'd woken up after our night at the garden rave to find an empty spot on the blankets beside me, the curtains dancing slowly behind me from the breeze sneaking in through a window we'd left open. I sat there on the floor for a while feeling lost and flat, a mixture of loneliness and the inevitable chemical come down. Deano came back to collect some things before going to his parents for the week, and Lauryn returned only to sleep before her night shift started. I found some Valium in Deano's room and took more than I should because I slept on and off for days. The sun rose and fell more than once and I drifted in and out of consciousness.

When my mobile screamed and vibrated beside my head, my first instinct was to make it stop. I answered before I had a chance to check who was calling and instantly regretted it.

'What the hell are you playing at?' Mum's voice shrieked down the line.

'What - ?'

'Don't you 'what' me. I've left you about a hundred voice mails and texts. I even had to phone the college. Where have you been? What about your course? What - ?'

'Mum, please...' I groaned.

'I've been worried sick. And then your mentor tells me you left your course over a month ago! Have you got into trouble?'

'No, Mum. I'm fine.'

'Then why haven't you called? What's happened?'

'I've been busy.' I knew it was a feeble excuse but my brain wasn't in full-functioning mode.

'Well you're not the only person in the world, Scarlet. I have other things to worry about, I don't need this as well. What on earth's going on?'

I hesitated, desperately wanting to block out the exasperation in her voice but not knowing how.

'I'm going to sort myself out. I'll start another course. Or I'll get a job.'

Truthfully, I had no plan. I didn't know what I was going to do. At first that had been liberating, but right now it just felt worryingly uncertain.

'I just don't know, Scarlet.' Mum's voice was strained and I could picture her pacing the kitchen tiles, anxiously rinsing out dish cloths and wiping down cabinets. 'You seem to be letting it all slip away. Why do you insist on fighting against everything? Why can't you just -'

'What? Do whatever you you want me to do?' I snapped.

'You've changed,' she said quietly, 'You're wasting so many good opportunities. And for what?'

I couldn't bare that tone, dripping with disappointment. I knew she thought I was failure, and maybe I was. I listened to her babbling on and felt like I was twelve again. Mum had just walked in and found me and my friend Lucy from down the street smoking weed in my bedroom. She freaked out and called her Mother because she'd never encountered drugs in her life and thought it was as bad as smoking crack. I tried to say sorry but she wouldn't listen and we had to sit round the table and have this big meeting. She kept shouting 'My own child! Marijuana!' and I tried to tell her it barely even counted as a drug but she didn't get it. She never gets it.

'I just want to be left alone.' I said quietly in between her ranting. Mum fell silent for a moment.

'You pull yourself together.' she said eventually, 'I don't know what you're doing but it has to stop. I feel like you're drifting away.'

I suddenly felt shame envelope me and it was infuriating.

'Stop trying to make me feel like shit, you don't know anything.' I yelled down the phone.

'I do know that you're being selfish.'

I couldn't listen anymore.

'I've got to go. Bye.' I said bluntly.

She didn't reply and I hung up. I pulled the duvet up to my neck and closed my eyes. I wouldn't admit to myself that she probably had a right to be worried. I was tired, and lonely, but I couldn't afford to overthink things. I just needed to feel good again, for that rush of energy to make me feel like I could take on the world. That would get me by. But it was Monday and our usual dealer had nothing left after the weekend.

I checked my phone again. No messages. I text Jamie for the third time that day.

Can you call me pls? S x

As I lay on my back in the dark room I could feel my throat burn as I lit a cigarette. My bones ached and I had the hint of a fever. I hoped I wasn't catching the flu. Remembering I couldn't recall the last time I ate, I padded into the kitchen and opened and closed cupboards aimlessly. I didn't want food. I wanted a line. So instead I filled a glass of orange juice and took a multivitamin. That should keep the flu at bay. I fell back into bed, my limbs still heavy from the Valium, and a heavy drowsiness overtook once more.

I almost leaped out of bed when my phone rang sometime later. It screamed at me from my bedside table and I tried to make out the screen through bleary eyes.

Jamie.

'Hello.' I croaked.

'Hey.' His voice was warm, wrapping me up in a soft blanket after days of loneliness and anxiety.

'What are...where are you?'

'Round the corner,' he said. 'Can you get any coke?'

It was 5am. I paused and felt a wave of irritation.

'Not at this time. I'm fine, thanks for asking.'

'Sorry babe, I'll be at your door in two minutes. Let me in.'

The phone went dead and I quickly pulled on my dressing gown. I pattered down the hall and swung the door open.

'Where have you been?' I looked at him, his twinkly eyes that looked like they were always laughing, and searched them for answers.

'What do you mean?' He tried to kiss me on the cheek but I pulled back. He frowned at me and put his hands around my waist.

'You disappeared.' I said, my voice already softening as I felt his hands on me.

'I had work. And I wanted to lay low in case Luke finds out I've been coming here.' he explained softly.

'Then you should have text me. Who cares what Luke thinks anyway?' I frowned.

'Look, it's difficult. I don't want to cause trouble.'

He wouldn't even hold my hand in public. I didn't know how much longer this could go on for. He tilted his head to the side and poked me playfully in the ribs.

'Stop.' I said, 'It's not funny. Can you be serious for once?'

'Oh, come on.'

Suddenly he scooped me up in both arms and carried me down the hallway. I wriggled but made little effort to resist, and squealed as he dropped me on my bed.

'You drive me nuts.' I shook my head as he lay down beside me, his head resting on his hands.

'I know.' he grinned, 'And you love it.'

The top few buttons of his shirt were open and I was drawn in by the intoxicating scent of his cologne. I pulled him close and and kissed him, hard. Instantly I forgot about my raw throat and aching limbs. He was always my cure and I was powerless against it.

'We should move away somewhere.' he whispered in my ear. 'Then it'll just be me and you'

'When?' I asked, stroking the back of his neck.

'Soon.' he promised.

That's all I wanted. Me and him, and our crazy world of love, sex and drugs. Then the party would never have to end.

The room was dark but I could see the outline of his face close to mine from the glow of the early morning sun.

'I missed you.' I said, burying into his chest as my arms wrapped around him.

We lay in silence for a few minutes with nothing but the steady sound of our breathing. Then Jamie sat up and started tapping away on his phone.

'Could we get any gear?'

I was jolted out of my state of blissful calm.

'Probably not till tomorrow.' I sighed.

I'd already gone through every option in my head, sent out about twenty text messages, and knew there was no way of getting it at this time of the morning. I was hoping he could stay with me and sleep until I could get some again.

‘I won’t be here tomorrow.’

‘Why?’

‘Work stuff. Come on, there must be a way. We’ll get wasted, just us. Deano must have some around here.’

I thought for a moment. There was a small chance Deano had left some here at the flat, but I really didn’t feel good about taking it. Although, if it meant keeping Jamie here with me, and I replaced it...

‘Okay, let me look. He’s at his parents, but sometimes he keeps a batch in his room. I suppose he wouldn’t mind if we had just a little.’

‘Brilliant. That’s my girl.’

As I opened Deano’s door I immediately looked around as if he might still be there. I knew that if he had anything it would be in his sock drawer. I crept across the room, stepping carefully over clothes and empty crisp packets. Fumbling around underneath his boxers and socks I felt a wave of guilt. Then a small, jagged ball formed beneath my fingers. I pulled out the little piece of scrunched up tinfoil and quickly opened it up like a kid with a Christmas present. I dabbed my finger on the white powder inside, my heart racing with excitement, and tasted it. Definitely coke. And good coke at that. Before I could let myself think about what I was doing I rammed the drawer shut and scurried back to my bedroom.

Jamie had put the lamp on and was sitting up in my bed.

‘Get it?’ he raised hs eyebrows expectantly.

'Yep.'

He grinned as I passed him the gram and watched him eagerly lay out some lines on the bedside table. As soon as the coke hit my system, all my senses switched on and the familiar rush of adrenaline raced down my spine. I was like a robot that had just been plugged in, the lights instantly flickering on from the inside out.

'Mmm...better.' I breathed.

Jamie's eyes sparkled as the coke hit him too and I entwined my fingers in his.

'Don't go to work. Just stay here, with me.' I pleaded.

'I can't, babe. I would if I could.'

I watched his pupils become wide from the coke and realised how much I loved the way he looked at me. He would always come back, because we'd created something that couldn't be broken.

'Deano's still being funny with me.' I told him as I lit a cigarette, 'pestering me about what I'm going to do in the new term. He's almost as bad as my Mum. This summer was supposed to be about forgetting all that.'

'Ignore him.' Jamie reached out and took the cigarette out of my hand. 'He's just jealous. You don't need him.'

'Well, he's one of my best friends. I don't want to - '

'But he's not a friend if he's making you feel like shit.'

I shifted uncomfortably, trying to form the right words.

'I just wish you two got on,seriously.'

'The only person I care about getting on with is you.' He pulled me towards him until our faces were almost touching. 'Because you get me.'

'Yeah,' I smiled, 'I get that you're an infuriating, but devilishly handsome, man who wakes me up at 5am to get wasted.'

'You wouldn't have it any other way.' he grinned. 'Another line?'

'Yes.' I said, 'I don't know how you do it.'

'Do what?'

'Manage to party so much.'

'Come on.' he laughed, 'You're just as bad. We can sleep when we're dead.'

The party never ended with Jamie. Maybe that's why I clung to him so much. His energy kept me addicted to him, as exhausting as it was sometimes. It made me feel alive just to be near him, I never wanted to give that up.

We lay there and talked about our tripping journey in the park, the people we met. My bed had became a sanctuary of sorts. Our secret cave shrouded in the dull light of the table lamp and a handful of candles that cut us off from the outer glare.

'You're cold.' Jamie ran his fingers over my hand.

'We ran out of heating. I'm okay.'

I'd actually started to sweat thanks to the gear. I tried to sniff but my nose was blocked and stinging. Jamie handed me a scrunched up tissue and I tried to blow out the contents.

'Gross.'

The tissue was stained with clumps of blood and other unidentifiable substances. Jamie peered at the bright red mess and frowned.

'Do you have any shot glasses?' he asked.

I looked at him skeptically. 'I don't think I'm in any fit state to start drinking right now.'

'No,' he continued, clambering off the bed and heading to the kitchen. 'For hot shots.'

A few minutes later he returned with two shots of hot water mixed with blackcurrant juice. He tapped out a small amount of coke into each and handed one to me.

'Cheers.'

We downed them quickly and I was relieved I didn't have to use my nose. It probably wasn't that great for my stomach either, but it was much easier right now. After just two more shots the coke ran out and the sun's rays crept through the gap in the curtains. Suddenly it became very quiet, that dull, empty feeling you got when you knew the drugs were all gone and there was no clear idea of where or when the next lot was coming. I lay on Jamie's shoulder and felt reassured somewhat by his closeness. I reassured myself that he'd be there for me when I needed him, during every high and every come-down. But I also needed him to tell me.

'Are you okay?' I said after a while, lifting my head to look at him. It was about all I could muster, I just couldn't find the words.

His eyes were closed but I could tell by the rise and fall of has breathing that he was still awake and listening.

'I'm great, beautiful.' he said quietly.

I paused for a moment and traced my finger over his lips. He softly kissed the tip. I opened my mouth again to speak, then thought better of it.

'Never mind,' I whispered to myself, resting my head back down on his shoulder, and it was quiet again for a moment.

'I love you too.' he said.

And right then and there, that was all I needed to know.

I must have drifted off. It was dark but I couldn't be sure of the time. Stretching my arms above my head, a flow of blissful contentment passed through me as I remembered those words Jamie had said. I turned to wake him.

But there was a cold, empty space in the bed where he'd been, the blanket tossed to the side. I sat up and my stomach sank as I peered around the semi-darkness. The flat was drenched in silence, thick and heavy this time, only the clock breaking it with careful ticks.

He was gone.

CHAPTER 9

I woke for the third time that night, shaking and drenched in sweat. I dreamed he was gone, only to wake and realise it was true. It had been over two weeks. Jamie had promised he'd come see me last weekend but he didn't show. There had been a couple of texts here and there, but now, nothing.

He haunted me, even during the day. At night I'd close my eyes and see his face. When I was with him I couldn't get enough, and when I wasn't I needed him with a desperation I never knew existed. If I lost him forever, I'd be gone with him, and I wasn't sure there'd be much of me left. Nothing worth leaving, anyway. He was draining me slowly, absorbing all I had until all I felt was emptiness. I was addicted to him, and I the detox was killing me.

A few days before I'd had a nightmare, not for the first time. We were all in a forest, Enya, Lauryn, Deano, Cian, Enya. I saw a figure pass through the shadows and heard his voice call my name. Everyone was talking, laughing, oblivious.

'Jamie!' I yelled out.

But there was nothing except blackness and trees that glared down at me menacingly with twisted branches.

Then I saw him again, the flash of his jacket buttons, and ran into the darkness.

'Jamie!'

I spun around and he kept disappearing. Every time I thought I caught up with him he appeared in another direction. The branches whipped at my clothes and scratched my skin.

Eventually I collapsed on the ground and curled myself tightly into a ball. The wind howled and I waited for the trees to consume me.

And then, out of nowhere, he was there. He stood over me, still, and I wasn't sure if he'd even seen me lying there.

'Where have you been babe?' I sobbed as I pulled myself up and searched his face.

'Right here.' he said, but he looked right through me.

Confused, I reached out my hand to touch him. But he began to evaporate through my fingers until there was nothing left but me and the black, evil trees.

At this point I woke, choking on my tears and struggling to breathe.

Now, after another night of broken sleep I watched the curtains move slowly back and forth in eerie silence. The nights had become warm, humid almost. I kicked the duvet around my feet restlessly and reached for my phone under the pillow. There was no coke left after last weekend. Deano had been away at his parents for a while and seemed to be slowing down a little, which meant there was even less coke available. The university finance people had overpaid me, my grant should have been stopped by now but an installment had hit my account. Of course, I'd withdrawn it immediately. Now there was around £30 left. I didn't think about them finding out, I'd pay it back eventually if I had to. I found Jamie's number in my phone and listened to it ring out.

Once, twice.

The only two times he had called last week were only at crazy hours when I least expected it. *Answer the phone*. I couldn't let him break the bubble. We were safe inside it, and reality was a notion that scared me more every day. I didn't care that our dream-world was fueled by drugs and fantasies and socially unacceptable behaviour. I needed it and I'd do anything to preserve it. All I needed now was something to bring me out of that place of total emptiness.

I heard his voice mail for the hundredth time and anxiety knotted in my stomach. I lay staring at the ceiling and sighed in exasperation when I heard a quiet knock on my door.

'Scarlet?' Lauryn said softly 'Are you ok?'

I sat up.

'Yes, fine. I'm fine.'

She pushed open the door and peered around for me in the darkness.

'Why's it so dark in here?' She flicked on the light and I scrunched up my face at the uninvited brightness.'What's going on?'

She was just home from a night shift, her eyes weary.

'I didn't feel too well.'

'I'm worried about you.'

I didn't meet her eyes. 'I'm okay, honestly.'

But she wasn't convinced.

'Have you heard from Jamie?'

I tensed at the sound of his name.

'No.' I said quietly. And then emotion bubbled over, overwhelming me. 'I hate him, Lauryn. I hate him for doing this to me and I hate that I still feel like this about him.'

She crossed the room and sat beside me on the bed.

'Maybe, I don't know...Maybe you should leave him to it.'

I knew what she meant. Let him go, forget all about him.

'I've tried.' I said helplessly.

'He doesn't deserve you.' Lauryn said, a hint of anger in her voice.

'I feel like I'm losing it, Lauryn.' I whispered, 'I'm scared. Everything's falling apart.'

'You don't have to be afraid.' she soothed. 'But you've got to slow down, before you make yourself ill.'

I stayed silent.

'Don't worry about me, Lolly.' I tried to sound strong, but she could see through me.

When she left I sat on the edge of my bed for a moment. The impulse for coke was unbearable, and I would give in to it without question, every time. Because now it had me in its grip. I was selfish. I was weak. I was a failure. But I didn't care. I kept imagining lining up the crystallized powder and feeling that intense tickle of excitement in my chest, seeping down my arms and filling every part of my body. I needed it. Now.

Automatically I pulled on a T-shirt and jeans, grabbed my laptop and swiftly crept out of the flat so Lauryn didn't notice. All the while a little voice in my head told me to stop, go back, I didn't need it. But I ignored it. I headed for the bus stop.

'Hi.' I said nervously as Dave the Dick opened the door and glared at me.

The stench of stale cigarettes and weed escaped into the street but it called me in because I knew what else was inside.

'What do you want?' he growled.

'Sorry,' I said 'I didn't have your number. I need something.' I spoke quietly so any passers-by didn't hear.

He nods towards the stairs behind him and I quickly follow him inside.

The bedroom was the same as before. Dark, smelly, filthy. Except this time we were alone.

'How many g's?' He sat down in his grubby chair and I tried not to meet his snake eyes.

'Well, this is the thing. I have £30 - '

'Fuck off.' he spat angrily, leaning forward. 'None of this arsing about again. You know how much it is.'

'But...'

'But nothing.' His eyes glowed like a dragon's and I fidgeted anxiously.

'This.' I thrusted my laptop towards him. 'Take this.'

He waved his hand dismissively.

'I haven't fucking got time for this, I've got proper customers waiting, like.'

'What else do you want?' I scrambled inside my bag frantically, waving the £30 at him and desperately rummaging around for change.

He fell silent and watched me intently for a minute until I stopped and shook my head helplessly. I was so close to relief.

'Maybe there's something I want.' He said suddenly, and the tone in his voice made my stomach drop.

'Like what?' My voice was shaky and I didn't meet his eyes.

Dave the Dick took a long draw of his joint before taking a large, clear bag from his jacket pocket in which there were lots of smaller bags. He carefully selected out several of the little ones and held them out in his hand.

'Suck my dick and I'll give you ten g's.'

I felt a wave of nausea as I saw him smirk to himself. I opened and closed my mouth and glared at him furiously. He knew he had me trapped, and I already hated myself for considering the offer. I thought of Jamie...he wouldn't care. We weren't even a real couple anyway. I thought of Lauryn, how horrified and disappointed she'd be if she found out. Then I thought of the misery waiting for me at home, lonely, drug-less, empty. Ten grams. That was about £500 worth.

'Fine.' I said before my brain could let it process any further.

Dave chuckled to himself in sick amusement and I felt sick.

'Five before, five after.' he winked, handing me the precious bags. I quickly stuffed them into my pocket.

He unzipped his trousers and clasped his hands behind his head, waiting.

'Get on with it, then.'

And then I was in robotic mode. I dropped my bag and sank to my knees. Suddenly I wasn't in my own body anymore. I watched from above as a girl gave some grubby looking guy a blowjob, her eyes clamped shut and her body rigid. All she thought of, in those few minutes that seemed to last a lifetime, were those special little bags in her left pocket.

Luckily, it didn't take long and I managed to bring my awareness back into the room so I could make a quick escape. Dave exhaled loudly in satisfaction.

I waited for him to give me the other five g's, wiping my mouth and suppressing the urge to vomit all over his filthy room. He threw three at me.

'That'll do you. It wasn't the best I've had.' He grinned and I wanted to lay into him right there and then, to pummel his disgusting, dirty face until there was nothing left but fleshy pulp.

But I didn't say a thing as I grabbed my things and heard him laugh smugly to himself as I ran out of the door. My hands shook and I gulped back the fresh air to try and steady my breathing. I wouldn't even think about what I'd just done, I'd already decided. I couldn't. Instead I thought of the amount of coke I'd accumulated and my shame was overtaken by relief. Relief and wonderfully giddy anticipation.

As soon as I got home I went straight to my room and shut the door. I laid out the bags, eight in total, and looked at them in awe. He'd promised me ten, but it didn't matter. I was practically inundated with coke, more than I'd ever had before. I could build a fucking house made out of coke if I wanted to.

I spent the day sniffing line after line, dancing around my room to house music. I even tidied up a bit. I promised myself to make it last as long as possible. But I wanted the first gram all to myself, to revel in the pleasure it sent through my mind and body. I was alive again.

The first one disappeared pretty fast. I hid six of them in my knicker drawer, my secret, prized treasure. Then I went straight to Lauryn's room with another clasped in my hand.

'Hey, Lolly.' I poked my head round her door. She was dozing on top of her bed covers, still in her work clothes.

'Oh, hi. You look better.' she said, bleary eyed.

She sat up and I went and plonked myself beside her.

'Look what I've got for us.'

I produced the gram of coke, dangling it in front of her like a carrot.

'How'd you get that?' She smiled and inspected the amount.

'The college overpaid me. I bought it the other day.' It was a half-lie. That money was long gone.

I quickly laid out some lines and we hoovered them up.

'So, are you coming to Enya's tonight? She's having a wee party.' Lauryn said, now awake and alert with a newfound energy.

'Why not?'

I couldn't have comprehended going anywhere earlier, but now I was rejuvenated. The only thing that gave me a dull ache in my chest was thinking about Jamie. But the coke had not only got me high, it had given me fresh optimism. He would call. Or he'd turn up. He had to.

Later that night, Lauryn, Deano and I stood in Enya's kitchen as a steady flow of guests arrived. The house vibrated with the beat of music and the air was filled with rambling voices and the clink of glasses. The three of us lingered in a corner of the kitchen, quietly observing the sequence...people arriving, making their introductions, cracking open beers. It seemed like all the parties were blurring into one.

I decided to put my drink in the fridge and wandered past the a group of long-haired guys in dark clothing. Just as I reached for the fridge handle, Enya appeared beside me.

'Hi, Scarlet.' She smiled thinly.

'Oh, hi.' I was growing tired of conversation. For once I'd just like it to be quiet. 'How are you?'

'Good, thanks.' she slowly exhaled smoke and looked at me curiously. 'How's it going with Jamie?'

I really wished she'd fuck off.

'Fine.'

'That's good to hear.' she took a draw of a joint and offered it to me but I shook my head. 'He seemed to be in a good mood when he was over the other day.'

I didn't look at her but I knew she could sense my irritation. Apparently Jamie hadn't disappeared off the face of the earth, although I didn't understand how he'd managed to visit her and Cian when he couldn't even be bothered to call me. Enya was pushing my buttons and I began to wonder why I'd ever liked her. Muttering some excuse about needing to to find my fags I returned to Deano and Lauryn. Deano was unusually quiet.

'What's up?' I asked him.

'Nothing.' he muttered. I raised an eyebrow. 'Really, nothing?'

We sipped our drinks in silence for a moment.

'So, this old lady at work -' Lauryn started.

'Do you know if anyone's been in my room while I've been away?' Deano interrupted.

We shook our heads.

'Why?' Lauryn asked.

'I thought I had a gram of coke in my drawer, but I can't find it.'

My stomach dropped as I realised I'd completely forgotten to replace the gram Jamie and I had shared.

'Um...' I mumbled and felt the colour rise in my cheeks.

'What?' Deano looked at me accusingly.

'I forgot. I took it the other week and I was going to tell you but it just slipped my mind and -'

'Where did you take it? At home?' He demanded.

'Yeah...'

'By yourself?'

'Well, no. Me and Jamie -'

I saw red hot anger bubble up in Deano's eyes.

'That's it.' he said, slamming his beer down on the side. 'I'm fucking done.'

'Done with what? Look, I'm sorry. I'll replace it.'

'It's not just that, Scarlet, and you know it.' His voice was filled with a frustration, a fury I'd never heard in him before.

'What are you talking about?' I asked, beffled.

'You don't see what you're doing? What a mess of things you're making in the name of 'freedom'?' he spat.

'What do you -'

'You're not free, Scarlet. You're trapped, just like the rest of us. At least we have the guts to admit it. It's all a big game to you.'

'I'm not trapped. I have plans. Me and Jamie...' I yelled back. People were starting to look, or drift out of the room in awkward silence.

'Fuck Jamie! You don't have plans, you have fantasies. You're living in a dream world. This time next year you'll be right here, in the same place doing the same old shit, if you don't get your act together.'

'And what's so fucking terrible about that? I'm happy.' I felt the hot tears well up in my eyes.

'And therein lies the problem. You can't even see it. You're happy? You sure don't look it. You're a mess, and you're heading for one almighty crash.'

'Fuck you, Deano.'

I spun on my heel and ran upstairs into the bathroom, Lauryn right behind me. I threw the toilet seat down and sat with my head in my hands as she closed the door behind us. Big, heavy tears rolled down my cheeks until my face was smeared with mascara.

'Don't cry. He didn't mean it.' Lauryn said quietly, crouching down beside me and offering me her bottle of vodka.

'Yes, he did.' I sobbed, wincing as I glugged back the bottle.

She gently rubbed my back as I tore off some tissue paper and tried to wipe my face, but it kept tearing and making it worse.

'Here.'

Lauryn rummaged in her bag and pulled out a face wipe and began carefully wiping under my eyes.

'He hates Jamie because he's jealous. He talks so much shit.' I said angrily.

'He's just worried about you.'

'No he's just being a know-it-all, as usual. The next time I see Jamie I'll tell him -'

'Scarlet,' she looked at me carefully and her voice was firm. 'Jamie's not coming back. You need to forget about him.'

I stared up at her. 'Yes, he will. He's just busy...'

Her eyes were sad and she looked at me with pity, which just made me feel worse.

'You're not good for each other. You're like two explosive devices waiting to go off.'

'For fuck's sake, not you too.' I shook my head and stared at the floor, 'I don't need a lecture.'

At that moment there was a quiet knock on the door.

'Scarlet.' Deano said quietly. 'I'm sorry. I didn't mean that.'

'I don't want to talk about it.' I said to Lauryn, 'Just go. I want to be on my own.'

'But -'

'Really, just go.' I insisted.

She sighed and left me alone with the bottle. I heard their voices grow faint as they went downstairs and then got up to make sure the bathroom door was locked. I sank to the floor and knocked back several more gulps of vodka. I was beginning to feel drunk, slow, numbed. It was exactly what I wanted, to cancel out the awfulness with chemicals. Maybe they were right. Maybe Jamie was never coming back, and maybe I was making a mess out of everything. I just couldn't bare the thought. Things were spiraling, fast, but there was a sick button in me I always had an urge to press. One that would detonate and cause me to crumble even further. I was too far away from normality now, the only path I could see was the one leading to further and further destruction, pushing the boundaries until there were none left to push. How could something so beautiful turn so ugly? Not so long ago I'd felt like we were all in it together, that we were sharing something wonderful. Now even my best friends were beginning to feel like strangers. I was dissociated, I was losing control.

I sat there for a while, listening to the alien sounds of music and laughter downstairs and never feeling more alone. Then someone started hammering on the door.

'Open up! Some of us need to piss!'

It was one of Cian's friends. I finished the vodka and pulled myself to my feet. As I stumbled out of the bathroom the guy looked at me skeptically. I ignored him and felt my way to one of the bedrooms. As I collapsed onto the bed, a figure groaned beside me. Some guy had passed out there but I didn't care. I curled myself up into a ball on the edge of the bed and felt the room sway. Round and round, round and round.

Chapter 10

I carefully tilted my head to the left and back again, concentrating intently on my reflection in the bathroom mirror. Something was different. I had definitely lost some weight, my cheek bones were sharper. And the dark circles around my eyes meant I was rocking the undead look. I ran my fingers steadily through my hair, which had recently become limp and lost some of its shine. But there was something else I couldn't quite put my finger on. I looked tired, like some of the fire had seeped out of me. After the party at Enya's, Deano had came upstairs and shared some of his coke with me. We didn't speak about our argument, but it was his way of saying sorry. The coke had pulled me out of my drunken stupor and I started to feel better. We were still altogether, and we didn't need to talk about any of that stuff. We just needed to plaster over it with a cocaine band aid and everything would be okay. At least, that's what we told ourselves. And, three days later, it was still working.

I shrugged and patted on some powder before heading back down to the living room. Deano was frying bacon in the kitchen while Lauryn lay on the carpet, earphones in and oblivious to the world. I curled my lip and frowned at the thick, smokey stench.

'Don't turn your nose up at my food. You're gonna be eating it.' Deano said firmly, after catching my look of disgust.

'I'm not hungry.' I replied, sitting down cross-legged next to

Lauryn, 'Have you got any coke left?'

'Not for you, no.' He flipped the crisped, sizzling slices of meat out of the pan and onto bread loaded with about three layers of butter. I sighed like a petulant child, 'But, if you eat this, I've got something else.'

'What?' I peered at him curiously, trying not to look too eager.

'Never you mind.' he handed me the plate and I eyed it apprehensively. Deano sat on the couch and took a huge chunk out of his own sandwich. I paused, looking from the dreaded sarnie back to Deano.

'Fine.'

I suppose I didn't want to look too emaciated, especially when I had to go home and visit Mum at some point. The thought made my stomach churn more than the bacon. I wish she'd stop pestering me and leave me alone. Just because she was bored and lonely, it didn't give her the right to encroach on my world with the persistence of a needy child. Every time my phone beeped, it was like a crude knife that splintered my life here like broken wood. Maybe I was being selfish. All I knew was that with every text or missed call I withdrew further from her and everything I used to think was real.

And still the pressing issue lingered over my head like a bad smell. I hadn't heard from Jamie. I wanted to assume he was busy with work, had been called away to an important events conference abroad, or even temporarily abducted by aliens.. I didn't want to tie him down, not really. I knew he was a free spirit too and could not be caged, but I just wanted him to stand still with me for a minute. It wasn't something I could talk to Lauryn and Deano about anymore. I knew they thought he wasn't coming back, that he'd left me and found someone else. But this was just how things were, how he was. He would be back, I told myself, he just needed his space. He always came back.

Deano devoured the remains of his sarnie and licked ketchup off each finger with enthusiasm. Several crumbs had settled in his beard and it irritated me that he couldn't see them.

'What do you have then?' I urged, diverting my attention away from the brown curls that framed his mouth and the anxious chattering in my brain.

He paused and eyed my plate to check that I'd at least attempted the sandwich, which had mainly resulted in me idly chewing pieces of bacon and moving it around the plate. But he could sense I was in no mood for messing around.

'Ketamine.' he said matter-of-factly.

'Horse tranquilizer?'

'Technically, yes.' he paused. 'But for recreational human-use - '

'I saw Mick Drysdale on Ketamine. He thought he was a flower.' I said bluntly.

'Yes, and I'm sure he very much enjoyed being a flower.' Deano grinned.

'He went and sat in the garden pouring mud over himself for three hours. They almost called his Mum.'

Deano chuckled. 'Well, it could have been worse.'

'What if it is?' I'd generally heard some not-so-great stories about Ket and I didn't want anything that may make me feel worse than I did. But when there were limited options...I bit my lip and looked at him thoughtfully. How bad could it be? Once again, reckless impulsivity was getting the better of me. My finger was hovering tentatively over the self-destruct button and it was urging me to press it. 'A tranquilizing effect does sound good right now.'

'I don't want any.' Lauryn perked up. I hadn't even noticed her take her earphones out. 'I've got work tomorrow. And it sounds too weird.' She scrunched up her face in distaste.

'Up to you.' Deano shrugged.

'Let's do this then.' I just wanted to get anything in my system right now.

I hadn't slept in days but the last lot of coke had ran out last night. Anxiety and restlessness had set it. I knew I was on the verge of an almighty comedown and it had been so long since I'd had one that I feared I actually wouldn't be able to hack it.

At that moment, Deano's phone pinged and he frowned as he looked at the screen.

'What is it?' Lauryn asked.

'Marty, he's at Johnny's rave.' he shook his head, 'Apparently a batch of dodgy E's are doing the rounds. Three people taken to hospital tonight.'

'Shit.' I uncurled my legs from their position and sat up.

'It's a good thing we only get them off Cian.' Lauryn said.

'Yeah. The more of these stories I hear about scumbags selling dodgy pills, the less I trust anyone. Just make sure you spread the word and only buy stuff from Cian. Or Enya.' Deano said.

'Roger, boss,' I saluted him. 'Now, let us proceed with the...horse stuff.'

He grinned and shook his head.

'Brace yourself.'

My last memories of normality were distant and fragmented now. Random snippets of Deano tapping out a small pile of brownish-white powder onto my old Prodigy CD case. Me asking why it was that colour. The brief moment of stomach-churning, yet thrilling, anxiety that I thrived on as I realised I had no idea what was going to happen. Like a movie where you reach the penultimate scene and all the loose ends are about to come together. Well, I didn't have long to wait. And instantly I knew there was not going to be a happy ending. That fizzling rush of adrenaline was replaced by an all-consuming sense of impending doom, and by that stage it was too late. It was the kind of fear that engulfs you when you're six and your parents are separating and you realise Dad's never coming home. Or when spend yet another sleepless Sunday night thinking about the meaningless week that is about to roll around and the fact that your life is stuck on pause, but amplified by a million. Invisible demons and hidden entities pushed and pulled me left and right as I was rapidly sucked into a bottomless void. I felt myself leaving the room, and I resisted with everything I had because I knew it would take me to a bad place.

But it was too strong. The sofa, Deano, the plate covered in bread crumbs and left over bacon fat, they were all there but through a blurry glass screen. I wanted to go home, wherever that was.

Someone once described hell to me as an eternal fall into the abyss. I couldn't tell if that memory was creating it, or I had simply arrived as the Devil's gates. Vomit spewed and splattered, catching and burning in my throat. Then the cycle would begin all over again, a rollercoaster ride that you couldn't get off, no matter how much you screamed. For fuck's sake let me off. I'm done, I thought, I'm sorry. I let things go too far and I have no one but myself to blame. Suddenly I was seeing the other side of the coin. This wasn't a game anymore, it was real. How could I have been so naive?

My eyes watered, my limbs were heavy as tree bark soaked in sticky winter dew. Just hang on, something told me. It was all I had, a vague hope that might not even exist. I gripped the floor as if it were the edge of the earth. It slipped and slided, laughing mercilessly at my feeble attempts to stay in reality. I was flying through space to the darkest corners of the universe, from heaven plummeting down to hell. The only connection to earth and life as I had known it was the vomit that continued to heave from my stomach. Maybe I was dying, and that might be okay. At one point I felt Lauryn grip my hand and heard her delicate, reassuring voice in my ear. But it was swallowed in an instant by the taunting blackness. The chittering voices voices were bad enough, the word 'she' echoing relentlessly on repeat. But it was the sinking, the constant fall into nothingness, that petrified me to the core. The thought of it never ending was more than I could bare. As the waves surged through me, I began to hear my own voice.

'Help me, Laur - '

'I'm here, don't worry.' Her voice danced through the blackness like angel wings, but it couldn't pull me out. Not yet.

I'd almost resigned myself to the oblivion, but the instinct to survive kept me locked in pergatory. *Just hang on, just hang on.* A thousand lifetimes passed, and suddenly I began to get my footing. I was slipping in and out, over and over. But in weak drips and drabs, almost as steadily as it had begun, I returned.

'Jamie...' my voice had started to connect with the instructions from my brain.

'It's ok,' I could see Lauryn now, her eyes wide with concern, 'he's on his way with Cian, from the rave. They won't be long. Here.' She gently lifted me off the floor and I felt Deano at my other side. Their presence eased things a little. The spinning slowed, now bearable dizziness and muddied vision. The fall had finally stopped, and now waves of relief washed over me like clean, holy water.

'How long did...What time is it?' I mumbled, my voice still sounding distant and alien.

I couldn't be sure how long I'd been swimming in that hellish murky quicksand, but it had felt like a millennium. Hours at least.

'Half twelve.' Deano said, his voice calm but weary.

'On Monday?'

'No, Sunday.' Lauryn nodded in confirmation.

It had been about forty minutes since I'd sniffed the line of ket. I looked around, bewildered, and noticed that Lauryn had managed to keep the puke situation relatively under control with thick

Tesco bags and minimal splattering. She'd also managed to tie my hair back mid-vom to prevent my hair from becoming soaked.

'I'm okay, Lolly. Thank you.' I assured her, seeing her anxiously wringing her hands. 'I'm just glad you didn't take it as well. There would have been a right mess.'

'I didn't get a good feeling about it,' she said worriedly.

'Sorry dude, I shouldn't have given you any.' Deano said weakly. He'd obviously not had a great time either.

I lay on the carpet and curled into a protective ball.

'It's not your fault. I just didn't expect that.' I closed my eyes, still shaken, and listened to my heart returning to its normal rhythm.

'You K-holed badly.'

'Try everything once, eh?' I shrugged, minimalizing the intensity of what I had just experienced.

'It's not always like that, though. Your state of mind has a huge impact on your experience. I guess we should have thought it through more.'

I think Deano thought this information might make me feel better. It didn't. I just didn't want to talk about it. My limbs were still like lead, each minor movement felt like wading through a thick swamp. So much for being a tranquilizer. I was fucking traumatized.

The rap on the door made me flinch. When I realised who it was I used what little energy I had to to sit up. He was back.

'Is she alright?' I heard Cian ask uncertainly.

As Lauryn attempted to frantically explain the turn of events from an outsiders point of view, I felt Jamie sit down beside me. I could smell his sweet deodorant as he pushed the hair back from my face.

'You silly cow.' I looked up to see his face creased into a soft smile. 'That stuff is for horses. Not pretty girls like you.'

I instantly felt my body release tension as things started to become more familiar. The reliable buzz of his presence canceled out much of the previous confusion, and all I needed was for him to be near. He was always my remedy, I thought.

'Where did you go?' I toyed with the collar of his shirt and curled my hand around his cheek, trying not to let tears of relief sting my eyes.

'I'm here now.' he said.

'If anyone is looking pills, I've some bangin' E's here,' Cian announced crudely, surveying the room. He really had no sense of what was and wasn't appropriate.

'God, I definitely don't want anything else in my system right now, Jesus.' I shook my head.

'For once,' Deano chuckled, and I managed to point my tongue out at him.

The darkness which had engulfed me just minutes earlier had almost dissipated. A lingering uneasiness remained yet I put all my energy into blocking it out. I wanted to forget and get over it as soon as possible, like it had never happened. Going back to that place was not an option.

'I'll have one,' Lauryn chirped, her eyes verging on desperation. The same desperation I'd felt all too often. 'It's been a horrible tonight.'

'Maybe you should take it easy then,' Jamie rubbed her shoulder.

'I'll join you.' Deano piped up, 'I don't know about you, but it would definitely cheer me up.' Lauryn nodded in agreement.

'Happy days,' Cian poked around and produced two green pills with little crowns on them. 'Tenner each, guys.'

'Tenner? Is it me or are they getting more expensive yet the quality stays the same?' Deano said playfully.

'No,' Cian protested, 'my supplier says these are the best around at the minute.'

Deano shrugged, and both he and Lauryn washed the pills down instantly. Now I'd started to feel better, I felt a pang of envy. Maybe I should get one, too.

As I toyed with the idea, the Dr Who theme song suddenly blared from Deano's mobile. He huffed as he fumbled in his pockets and eventually found it.

'Hello - ' we all froze as a muffled but angry voice spat down the phone, 'Ye...Um...' Deano stuttered and struggled to get a word in. 'No, but...ok.'

He hung up the phone and shifted uneasily.

'Who the hell was that?' Jamie stood up.

'Well?' I urged.

'Luke.' Deano blurted out. The room fell silent.

'What...why?' I asked, bewildered.

'He must have got my number somehow. He said something about Jamie meeting him the other day.'

Jamie was quiet.

'What is he on about?'

'I don't know,' Deano babbled, 'but he sounds seriously pissed off.'

My head was dizzy with confusion. 'He's such an interfering knob. What's his problem? Give me the phone, I'm calling him back.' I reached out to grab it from his hand.but Deano jumped back.

'I don't think that's a good idea, Scar.'

'Why? I've had it up to here with his shit - '

'He's on his way over here.'

I stood rooted to the spot, my brain racing. Luke could be volatile, we all knew that. And no doubt he wouldn't have any qualms about throttling the guy who messed around with not only his sister, but his ex. We also had drugs in the flat, we couldn't afford any trouble or police at the door. The others bickered between themselves as I tried to think. Then, Lauryn's small voice carried through the noise.

'Scarlet.'

I turned around and saw her sitting upright on the edge of the sofa, hands gripping her knees. The look on her face made my stomach churn.

'Lauryn, what's wrong? Are you ok?' I knelt down beside her. Beads of sweat had begun to roll down her temples and the colour had drained from her cheeks.

'I don't feel right.' she whispered.

'It's ok,' I rubbed her hand, 'Don't panic. We'll get rid of Luke. You're probably just having an anxiety attack.'

Jamie moved over to me as I stood up, and I squeezed his hand. There was no point in running now. He would make this all alright, I trusted him. I watched him massage the back of his neck anxiously as I tapped my foot nervously against the sofa. There wasn't much time to figure out what to do. In one sharp sound, the doorbell rang.

Chapter 11

I looked at Jamie nervously and hoped he would take some form of control now. I could feel burning apprehension accelerate in my veins, and that all too familiar feeling that things were on the verge of spiraling. I desperately needed him to fix things, to put things right so it could be just like it was before.

The bell shrieked furiously over and over.

'You're going to have to talk to him.' Deano urged Jamie, who was now pacing the floor, his hands clasped behind his head. He frowned and studied the floor for a moment, before looking up at us.

'Okay,' he sighed, 'let's go.'

'We'll be right behind you.' Deano assured him as he and Cian stepped into the lift with Jamie.

I watched the metal doors close and heard the creak of the lift as it descended to the foyer. Immediately, I turned to Lauryn, who was still frozen to the sofa edge, her eyes fixed firmly on the floor. She was shivering now.

'Come on,' I said decidedly, wrapping a blanket round her shoulders, 'You'll be fine. You just need some air.'

I eased her up and made for the lift. I couldn't leave her. But I had to make sure Jamie was alright, that Luke saw we were in this together and nothing he could do would change that. My stomach churned as the lift took what felt like a year to reach the ground floor. With one arm around Lauryn I stepped out into the cold night air. I had forgotten my coat, but ignored the bite of the wind on my shoulders. Then the echo of harsh voices sliced the air and I froze. They were coming from the car park to the rear of the flats.

Turning the corner I saw Luke, his hand gripping the scruff of Jamie's t-shirt.

'Stop it!' I rushed towards them as Luke slammed him against the wall with a thud. Deano was making futile attempts to pacify him but Luke's eyes were lit with fury.

'Don't try the innocent act with me,' he spat, nothing except palpable hatred in his voice, 'You were big and clever enough to mess my sister around, let's see you play the big man now.'

A quiet, wavering voice mumbled in response, and it took me a moment to realise it had come from Jamie.

'I...I'm sorry...mate, I didn't - '

'Save it. I'm not your fucking mate. I know what kind of creep you are. How much of a mug do you think I am?'

'He's ten times the person you are, you dick. Now get off him.' I yelled.

Luke threw his head back and laughed.

'Really, Scarlet?' he sneered, 'You don't think he might only be interested in you for getting wiped off his face on drugs and having someone he can shag whenever he feels like it? This lad seems to have a consistent track record.'

'For god's sake, Luke - ' I started.

'Don't, Scarlet. You're a naive little girl, as much as you try not to act like it. You may be sucked in by him but I'm not.'

I waited for Jamie to jump in and start defending himself.. But he just stood there, his hands up in pathetic surrender, mumbling excuses and apologies like a kid who'd been caught stealing penny sweets. Luke roughly let go of Jamie's shirt and pressed his face close to his.

'Tell her, Jamie. Tell Scarlet about how you've still been sleeping with Amber, and not seeing your kid for months on end?'

My stomach felt like it had caught in my throat. What kid?

'Oh, she doesn't even know.' Luke laughed in astonishment when he saw my expression. 'This is great. Typical, really. You never see your own daughter and now Amber tells me you've been sleeping with her and then disappearing when you're supposed to have Kayla. You worthless piece of shit.'

Suddenly I remembered the photo of the little girl in Jamie's wallet, how he'd told me it was his niece. Luke was lying, he had to be. But the expression on Jamie's face told me all I needed to know.

'Scarlet.' Deano's voice came out of the darkness, loud and frightened.

I spun round to see him knelt down beside Lauryn, her tiny frame slumped against the wall. 'I think she's really ill.'

Even in the darkness I could see the deep concern etched on his brow. I rushed over to her and took her cold hand in mine, stepping past the thick pool of vomit at her feet. Her head flopped on my shoulder and I stroked her soft hair.

'What do you think we should - ' I stopped mid-sentence as my eye caught something through the hazy orange street light. Seeping off the curb in slow, heavy drips. The vomit, streaked with black blobs. I leaned forward and squinted. They weren't black. Even in the weak light I could make out the glisten of dark red blood.

'Deano.' I could hear the fear rising in my voice, 'She needs to go to hospital.'

Deano fumbled with his phone. Rain had started to lightly spit on us, but I knew she was too sick to make it upstairs. She continued to heave but nothing came out, just a dark stain left on her lips. The retching got worse, and I struggled to keep her from keeling over. It echoed violently across the dark car park.

'It's ok, Lolly. We're getting you to hospital.' I reassured her as I heard Deano jabbering away to the phone operator, 'It's probably just a bug.'

Enclosing my fingers tightly round hers, I realised I needed her just as much as she needed me right now. I wouldn't let go of her hand until all this was over.

Luke's voice still roughly permeated the air against Jamie's feeble responses, oblivious to our panic.

'Shut up!' I called out to them weakly.

The ketamine trip had left me weak and my limbs still felt incongruous on my body. That fear from before, the inescapable haunting that things were about to bubble over, began to erupt. But they didn't stop. Lauryn's eyes were blank, as if all the energy had been vacuumed from her, and Luke's voice grew angrier and hammered in my head until it became unbearable.

'Shut *up*!' I screamed, before loud, heavy sobs escaped my mouth and I turned to look at them in exasperation. 'Lauryn's sick. Really fucking sick. The ambulance will be here any minute.'

Luke stopped mid-sentence and fixed his black eyes on my tear-stained face, and then on Lauryn. Jamie shifted from one foot to the other, peering at the ground. He couldn't even look at me.

'I'll go.' he said suddenly.

'What?' I tried to search his face for answers, but he didn't look up. A sick sensation in the depths of my stomach told me if he left now he wouldn't be coming back. 'Where? I need you here.'

'I'm sorry, Scarlet,' he said casually, like it was the easiest thing in the world to say. 'Come on, Cian.'

'Sorry for - ?'

My body vibrated with anxiety. He couldn't go, not now. A deep ache began to settle in my bones, the kind of ache that dulls over time but never really leaves you. Disorientated, I felt panic scrape down my spine like razor blades and for a moment thought my organs might give up altogether. I watched Luke as Jamie looked up at him cautiously, rubbing the back of his head and motioning to Cian.

'I hope shagging Enya was worth missing your daughters birthday for. I waited with her and Amber for hours.' Luke hissed bitterly.

I wanted to throw up, but I was numb and confused. Luke looked down at Lauryn and concern spread across his face. Then his eyes fixed on Jamie, unwavering. Before I could muster any words, Jamie and Cian took off past us across the car park towards the main road. But not before Luke pointed in my direction and hissed after them, 'You stay the fuck away from Kayla from now on. You're no father.'

Jamie's face was blank. I wanted him to look at me. Just once.

But he wouldn't. His silence said more than any words could have. He hesitated for a moment, his hands shoved loosely in his pockets. A look briefly crossed his face, maybe guilt. But it was quickly replaced by that awful indifference.

And then he and Cian evaporated into the blackness.

As their footsteps faded into nothing, I felt my hand against the hard concrete as I crouched beside Lauryn. My insides had frozen, and I could barely comprehend what was happening. All I knew for sure was that my body was quivering in shock, and that trying to get my thoughts in order to decide what to do next felt like the most painful task in the world. I sat numbly, the sound of Deano's voice on the phone muffled and distant. Was he shouting at me? The pills. The ecstasy pills. What was he talking about? He was vomiting now. But between the retches I managed to make out what he was saying.

'I just got a text,' he rasped, 'It was Cian. He's the one that was selling the bad batch of E's. I've felt sick all night but they must have really disagreed with Lauryn.' He spat repeatedly and wiped his mouth on his sleeve before shoving two fingers down his throat. 'I'm getting this out of my system. That bastard.'

'Disagreed? Look at her!' I shrieked.

Cian. Surely not?

Everything was falling apart, piece by piece. Time started to slow, like I'd been swallowed back into the dark void, my arms flailing as I tried to hold on. Maybe I was still tripping on the Ketamine. Could this be real? My thoughts began to unravel at terrific speed, everything that surrounded me crumbling to rubble.

And then the blinding lights. Orange. Blue. Flashing furiously as a great monster roared round the corner. I could see my body now, slumped against the cold wall, black streaks of mascara running from my eyes and nonsensical sounds emerging from my mouth. Deano. Talking so fast to a paramedic that I couldn't understand him, his arms frantically waving about his head and his eyes wide. And Lauryn. Leaning heavily on my shoulder, her delicate hand still wrapped around mine. Why were they pulling her away? I wouldn't let go of her hand. I promised.

With one sharp jolt I was catapulted into panic as strangers yanked her off me and began chattering urgently in terms that were clinical and foreign. My voice was louder now, desperate and lost in the chaos. Lauryn's little frame began to seizure violently, like a rag doll being shaken by some cruel kid. *Make it stop. Make everything as it was before.* I couldn't bear it. I just wanted to keep hold of her hand because she needed to know I was there. A lady with a soft voice and sickly sweet perfume held me by my shoulders as I tried to get to Lauryn, fits still tearing through her and her eyes rolling around in her head like wild marbles. It didn't look at all like her, this wasn't my Lauryn.

Then it stopped. Her limbs went limp and a roaring silence settled momentarily. I was on my knees now, drained. But I just couldn't tear my eyes away from the scene playing out in front of me. One, two. One, two. A memory surfaced of a first aid class where they told us to do chest compressions in time with the Bee Gee's song, 'Staying Alive.'

One, two.

Staying alive, staying alive/

One, two. One, two.

I admit I still held on to something at that point, that invisible thing called hope that we cling to even when everything is lost. Even when they calmly stated the time of death. 01.14. But no, hope can be a dangerous thing. It was when I saw her eyes...those pale blue rings surrounding eerily wide pupils. Long, soft eyelashes framing a deadened gaze that was once angelic, pure and alive with laughter. That was when I knew. And nothing would be the same.

Chapter 12

So I guess that's how I ended up here. I should probably tell you what a crazy place rehab is, full of crack heads and awkward Narcotics Anonymous meetings. Or a cringe-worthy spa that you hear about celebs going to for 'a rest'. But no, this is on the NHS so it's not exactly swanky, although I'm told I'm very lucky to be here. I don't feel lucky. I feel like complete shit in it's worst form.

Really, this is a holding cell for all kinds of people that have lost their way in one way or another. Most of them seem normal enough, whatever that means, but then again I've barely left my bed so I wouldn't know. The staff are okay, I suppose. But the food is bad. Really bad. At this point my greatest desire is to be left the hell alone. Not poked and prodded by nurses or mentors trying to sift through my head and throwing around phrases like 'suicide risk' and 'personality disorder'. As if anything can help me now. There's a reason they call it a bin. It's a dumping ground for the failures, the useless and the forgotten.

I've been lying facing this wall for hours. There's a window to the left but I don't want to look out of it, so I just stare blankly at the grey, peeling paint and try not to think of anything but the the ridges in the brickwork. I don't know what time it is, and it doesn't matter. I pull the thin sheets over my head to try and block out the mindless chatter outside in the hall from other residents. How can everyone just go about their business like nothing has happened? My world has crashed to pieces, yet the world heartlessly carries on as normal. Maybe there are others in here whose world's had stopped, you just don't see or hear from them. As sick as it sounds, I sort of hope someone else is feeling the same way. Misery loves company.

It's during the night time that it all comes back. During the day there's always someone who wants to check your blood pressure or ask you that horrific question, 'How are you today?' But at night, the lights go out and there's this eerie silence. Someone comes and does a head count before bed to make sure one of us hasn't escaped or something. I always hear them coming and pretend to be asleep. I wait until the footsteps fade and quiet descends. It's then I think about Lauryn. I wonder where she is, and there's this vicious ache in my chest because I can't be sure she is okay. I can't protect her. I didn't protect her. And then I think about Jamie and a fury of emotion rushes through me so violently It's difficult not to scream out loud. What is left of my shattered heart breaks over and over again, every day. I fail to understand how the human body can withstand such trauma without some ghastly effect showing on the outside. I was wounded, bleeding and in agony, yet no one could see it. Not a thing. I guess that's why people cut themselves. I don't even have the energy to do that. Plus, they took all my 'dangerous' objects off me when I came in. Fair enough, I can understand the razors and the headache tablets. But my hair dryer? What am I going to do, blow-dry myself to death? Still, it doesn't stop me wanting to bash my head off the wall to try and rid myself of the shitty mush festering inside.

In a way I envy Lauryn, as bad as it sounds. She'll never again feel pain or loss or heart break. She will never have to confront her demons. We always said we would sleep when we were dead, and that life was for living to extremes. I hope she's sleeping now. By God, she needs it. Talking about her in the past tense seems unnatural. I still can't bring myself to remember those last moments, how confused and scared she must have been. It's unbearable that something so good and pure should be taken from a world that can be so awful and dark. To be honest, I can't make sense of any of it, and I don't know if I ever will.

There are five other women in the facility. I know if Lauryn were here she'd be giggling with me as we listened in on their conversations. Like today, there's a large woman of about fifty who is always pacing the floor and loudly complaining about not being able to see her counselor

'This is a fucking disgrace,' She's breathing heavily, like an impatient rhino. He face is always red. I think she's an alcoholic. 'I know my rights! All you people do is sit there and do nothing. I'll have my solicitor deal with this, don't you worry.'

'Aye, exactly. Your solicitor.' A meek woman who is as thin as a pole enthusiastically agrees, fueling that incessant pacing up and down the hallway.

'I won't be taken for an idiot. You think because I'm in here I don't have the same rights as anybody else?'

'You do, you do.' The younger woman nods excessively. You can tell just by her squeaky voice that she has that mousy brown shade of hair, wispy strands of it hovering chaotically round her face.

The big woman sounds sweaty, she's worked herself up into a right state. Every time she huffs and puffs, Mousy Brown spurs her on with her head-nodding and keen sounds of agreement. I know for a fact if Lauryn were here she'd be stifling giggles with her mouth all scrunched up. And I'd be grinning back, neither of us able to keep a straight face. She'd bring me in heaps of magazines and we'd sit and judge all of the awful outfits the celebs were wearing and scoff at how it should really be us being paid to party because we did it so well, not like those dull reality stars with too much fake tan. I miss her pretty laugh. I miss her soothing aura. Rationally I know she's gone, but some part of my brain hasn't caught up and I'm not even sure I want it to. See, the thing is, I don't know *where* she's gone. I've never thought much about life after death. I know I don't believe we all go floating around in heaven or hell, but a part of me wishes I did believe in all that. At least then I would know she was up there, because she would definitely not be in the other place. It's hard to believe we just vanish, all our traits, our wishes and our dreams, disappearing into oblivion until we're nothing but worm food. Truthfully, I don't want to think of it at all.

Another day nurse appears. It's Monday, so everyone has a physical check up and is tested for drugs. I probably pissed the last one off so much she refused to come back. This one is a bit older, maybe late thirties, and she marches right up to the head of the bed.

'Afternoon, love!' She's so cheery. It's so hard to be rude to people when they are genuinely cheery. 'May I be so cheeky as to take your blood pressure? Then I promise I'll not pester you for the rest of the day.'

I manage to lift myself up into a sitting position and she wraps the device around my arm.

'Have we eaten today?' she continues. I hate when people say 'we' when they mean 'you'.

I shake my head.

'Well it's important to eat, love. Can I make you some toast?'

'No, thanks.' I mumble.

'Some tea, then?'

'I said I'm not hungry.' I snap. I don't mean to sound so bratty. I'm just sick to high heaven of being offered tea, as if it was this magical, all-curing potion. 'I'm sorry. I'm just not feeling too well.'

'No need to be sorry,' she says softly 'Just do your best, that's all that matters really, isn't is?'

She's nice. I wish I could be cheery for her and smile and say all the things you're supposed to say. But it would be a lie, and I haven't got the energy.

After she leaves I patter down the end of the hall to the female toilet. The large lady and Mousy Brown are now deep in conversation outside one of their rooms. They pause as I walk past, my bare feet making sticky noises on the floor, then start up their hushed chatter again as I reach the bathroom and close the door firmly. There is no lock. Well, there is an attempt at a lock, but it doesn't work. Someone should really fix that. The toilet is a small room lit with unflattering yellow light, but I still get a shock when I catch myself in the mirror. God, I look like shit. My hair is sticking up in all directions and my skin is pale and blotchy. I know I let my appearance slide recently but I look like a total stranger. Like, basically dead. I can't bare it anymore so I focus on my hands and wash them a few times. Then a few times more. I don't know why.

I feel bad about being rude to the nurses. None of this is their fault. Not long ago I could look in the mirror and be okay with what I saw. Now, I just see a nobody. A bad person, a bad friend, a waste of space. It's like I've been mixed up in a blender, I literally don't know who I am anymore. I feel tears start to sting my eyes and quickly reach for the toilet paper to blot them away. I don't want to start crying, because I don't know if I'll be able to stop. Things are bad enough as they are, I don't want to be the frizzy haired girl who badly needs a bath sitting crying in the toilet of a rehab. That would be an awful stereotype.

One of the female staff members must have seen me go into the toilet because they knock on the door and tell me my Mum is here to see me. I can't get a moment's fucking peace. I've been expecting this, though. I take a deep breath and open the door.

Her face is strained. She's standing there clutching her brown leather handbag with both hands and her shoulders are tensed. She has that grey overtone to her skin, weathered from years of smoking, and her body slumps like a tired, old tree. Her shoulder length brown hair is pushed behind her ears and silver strands are appearing near the roots. I see her sad eyes and look away as a lump forms in my throat.

'Hi, darling.' she sighs.

Suddenly she falls forward and wraps her arms around me. We don't usually hug, but this time I squeeze her back and breathe in that distinct, comforting smell that only Mothers have. It brings me back to my childhood, racing round the garden at the height of summer and being scooped up in her arms. My eyes rapidly fill up and I clench them shut to try and stop them leaking.

'I'm sorry, Mum.' I say. It just comes out.

'I'm sorry, too.' she sniffs, pulling back and kissing my forehead.

'What are you sorry for?' I manage to hold back the tears.

'For failing you. As a mother.' She shakes her head and fiddles anxiously with the ring on he finger that she never takes off. I realise I've picked up the same habit.

'What do you mean? You haven't done anything wrong.'

'If I'd done things differently, you might not be here.' She keeps her eyes on the floor.

'That's not true -'

'But it is. I should have dealt with things...I should have been there for you more when your Dad left.' The words tumble out rapidly and I can feel the desperation in her voice. I stay quiet for a moment. We never talk about Dad. Mum gets all jittery and anxious and closes up like a clam. 'He broke my heart, Scarlet. I never got over it. But I should never have let it come between us.'

Then she looks up at me and my chest aches to see so much pain inside her.

'No, Mum.' I take her hand in mine and hold it tight so she knows I mean it. 'This is my fault, no one else's. I let things get out of hand. I put myself in here.' As I say it out loud I realise it's true.

'I've been selfish and reckless. And I'll fix this. I promise.'

Mum nods slowly but I know she still feels the weight of intense guilt. That just makes me feel worse. I want to keep my promises, but I'm torn between wanting to take her pain away and clinging on to what's left of...well, I'm not exactly sure what. I can't imagine a life without drugs and some dark part of me just won't let it go.

'I'll always blame myself, though. When you're a Mother, you'll understand.' she says in defeat.

'Well, don't worry. Things will be different.' I assure her. I want to say anything that will take the terrible expression off her face.

'And poor Lauryn. She was such a sweet girl. I was so scared, Scarlet. That could've been you. I can't bare the thought of losing you.'

'You're not going to lose me.' I tell her.

'Because you'll only get so many chances before you can't go back,' she urges. 'Don't waste them.' She says it as if she knows what she's talking about. She hesitates for a moment, then looks at me firmly.'Your Dad. He was a heroin addict, Scarlet. I tried to help him, I did everything I could. Then one day I gave him an ultimatum, it was either the drugs or me and you. He chose the drugs.'

I sit in shocked silence for a moment. I had no idea.

'Why didn't you tell me?' I say eventually.

'I wanted to protect you. I didn't want you to feel like someone had chosen that life over you. You were so little. No matter what I did, I couldn't help him, because he wouldn't help himself. But I loved him,' A tear rolls down her left cheek and her grief is palpable. 'I really loved him.'

I reach forward and wrap my arms around her.

'It's okay, Mum.' I whisper. 'You don't have to worry about me.'

And right now I really need it to be true.

Dr Shirley puts her pen to her lips and tilts her head in that annoying way people do when they think they've got you all figured out. She surveys me for a moment and I shift in my seat, somewhat miffed that she's making me uncomfortable. Her makeup is perfect, and her thick brown hair lays neatly around her shoulders. I guess she's not bad looking for a middle-aged woman. I wonder how she has the time to look so presentable when she has so many people's brains to be fixing. I think about making a smart comment telling her as much, but decide against it. We've succumbed to this awkward game where it's only a matter of time before one of us speaks. I don't give in. She wants me to look straight at her and bare my soul, let all of my personal rubbish fall out on her lap so she can tick her boxes smugly and feel like she's won. It's quiet for some time.

'Let's forget the labels,' she places her biro down on the table and crosses her legs. She's wearing those sheer tights that make your legs look all smooth. 'Why do you think you have a problem with drugs?'

'I don't have a problem.' I say bluntly.

'Using cocaine on almost a daily basis, not to mention the other substances you mentioned, Ecstasy, Ketamine, alcohol...does that not sound like a problem to you?'

'Well, I obviously didn't use ecstasy on a daily basis, that would be really stupid.'

'And taking cocaine isn't?'

'It's not the same.'

'You didn't answer my question.'

She was really starting to get on my nerves. You just can't talk to people about this stuff unless they've done it themselves. They never get it. They think everybody is the same and that we're all those stereotypical addicts that steal off their granny to pay for gear and sit in junkie houses all day.

'It's not a problem. Everyone else is making it a problem. My *problem* is I've lost my best friend and...It doesn't matter. This place is now my problem.' I say 'problem' so many times it starts to sound strange. I begin scratching the wooden table edge irritably, and the sound breaks the deadening silence in between our sentences.

'What do you feel when you take drugs? What makes you go back each time?' she continues.

'What does that have to do with Lauryn?' People hate it when you answer their questions with a question.

'It has a lot to do with Lauryn,' she says gently, 'You shared these experiences with her. You were using almost every day, and that lifestyle is sadly what led to her...'

'Shut up!' I surprise myself at how loud it comes out, 'Don't try and...that could have happened to any of us. She didn't deserve it. If anything I should be dead, not her.'

I barely notice the tears rolling down my cheeks as my voice cracks. Burying my face in my hands I suddenly feel very exposed. I want everyone to go away so I can hide under a blanket.

'I think that's enough for today, Scarlet.' Dr. Shirley pushes a box of tissues towards me and waits patiently with her hands in her lap for me to calm down, 'We'll meet again on Friday. In the meantime, get some rest. Your body and mind have been through a lot, now is the time to recuperate.'

Rest. I almost laugh. Her and her know-it-all tone. I told you what they're like. Rip you open then leave you to deal with all the mess.

I don't know how I get to my bed but I shut the door and crawl under the covers. Then some stupid member of staff comes in and opens it again, mumbling something about policy and being on observation. I lay there restlessly, my thoughts swimming, making it impossible to sleep. And that ridiculous question keeps resurfacing. *What do you feel like when you take drugs? What makes you go back each time?* I am so angry at myself for letting Dr. Shirley churn up all these horrible feelings that I've been working so hard to control. I'm on the verge of losing it. It's like that impending sense of doom when you're about to puke. Or maybe I am going to puke, I don't know. I just keep getting these waves of immense anger boiling inside that I don't know what to do with. Everything seems out of my hands, uncertain and out of control. Because it isn't just Dr. Shirley that needs an answer to that question. I do, too. It festers like a scratching beetle eating away at my insides. I think of Lauryn and Deano. I think of how we used to be, before. Still-frames of the past flash through my mind and I begin to lose the energy to fight them. Me and Lauryn getting lost on our first day on campus. Mum's fake smile as I leave for university, and the guilt I tried to suppress for abandoning her. Deano and I sniggering in the library and getting kicked out for disturbing the other students. They made no sense, but my head was rapidly trying to sift through it all to find an answer, and for some reason I couldn't let it go.

Realising I am too worked up to even attempt to sleep, I turn over and look around the lonely room with its pale blue walls. They're masked in a pale blue light sourced from a small window with a steel sill. There's a sink and a grey plastic chair with a few books and magazines on it, but aside from that it's so bare I almost can't stand it. I am pretty certain that nothing could incite any kind of happiness or interest in me right now, and I'm suddenly very scared. What if this is it? What if I never feel happy again? The thought fills me with a fear so intense it makes me dizzy. And what's worse, there's no one but myself to blame.

Before I can change my mind, I get up, put on my slippers and walk straight down the hall to the small office on the left. I knock on the door and open it before I'm invited.

'Scarlet, is everything okay?' Dr. Shirley stops packing her files into her brown leather case and looks at me, surprised.

'Yes...Well, no.' I suddenly don't know exactly how to get the words out.

'Sit down.' She motions to the chair but I don't move.

'You asked me why I took drugs, why I kept going back...'

'Yes, I did.' she says patiently.

'Well, I think it's because I'm scared...I don't know who I am without them. But I definitely know who I am with them. And I think that's why I go back, if that makes sense.'

'And do you like the person you are when you're on them?' she asks.

'I'm not sure. I used to.' There's a pause.

'This is good, Scarlet. It's not easy to admit you're afraid, and you're certainly not the first person to feel that way.'

I nod and chew my lip. As I go to leave I turn back to her. 'Have I ruined everything? I mean, will it always be like this?'

Dr. Shirley smiles. Kindly, not in that patronizing kind of way. 'No, not if you don't want it to be. This is your second chance.'

I thank her and leave, and as I walk slowly back to my room, I realise I feel a little less heavy than before.

Chapter 13

I sleep fitfully, despite being dosed to the eyeballs with Valium. Every time I reach semi-consciousness the anxiety, followed by crippling emptiness, begins to bubble in my stomach and only simmers down again once I drift off for another short while. Up and down, over and over. Like a damn record player on repeat. I feel the sweat that sticks the thin sheets to my skin and wriggle restlessly, unable to find a comfortable position.

'Scarlet.'

The sound pierces my skull like a dagger. She touches my shoulder and I jump as if I've been shot.

'There's a gentleman here to see you.'

It takes a few moments for me to get a sense of my surroundings. Incomprehensible groans escape my mouth as I attempt to raise my head off the pillow. A figure, dark and blurred, hovers at the end of the bed as the nurse disappears into the corridor.

'Hi.'

Deano stands awkwardly against the metal bed frame clasping a plastic bag. My stomach drops and I lay there, frozen. Hesitantly, he edges towards me as if I have the plague and places the bag beside me. I haven't seen him since that night. It feels like it's been years rather than a few weeks, and neither of us have a clue what to say. His presence unnerves me at first, a sharp reflection of everything I wanted to forget.

'I brought you some things...' he manages eventually and fumbles around in the carrier bag before producing a huge bar of white chocolate (my favourite), a few packets of cigarettes and a magazine.

'Thanks,' I say quietly. After a few awkward seconds that feel like a lifetime, I clear my throat.'Sit down.'

He perches on the edge of the bed carefully and starts to pick at his nails, staring intently down at his hands so he doesn't have to look at me. How on earth did we get here? This isn't us. I notice how tired his eyes are, the defeated slouch in his posture, and realise I'm not the only one who's been all used up. The most painful part, and probably what made it impossible to look at each other, was that we knew we'd done it to ourselves.

'When do you think you'll get out?' he attempts.

With tremendous effort I pull myself up and draw my knees to my chin, the scratchy blanket still twisted around my legs like ivy on a wall. My limbs are still heavy from the medication.

'I'm not sure. A few weeks maybe.'

'Oh.' He doesn't lift his head.

I try to break the tension by reaching out to take the chocolate, tearing open the packet and breaking off a piece. It's the first I've eaten in a day or so and the smooth square feels like an alien substance sliding down my throat. I wave the bar at Deano.

'Want some?' .

'No, thanks.' Deano's eyes briefly meet mine and it stings like salt in an open wound. 'I'm sorry I didn't visit before. It's been...with the funeral and all.'

'It's fine.'

He stares at the floor in silence. I can sense his nerves combined with a horrible flatness that seemed to have sucked the life right out of him.

'Have you heard from Jamie or -'

'It doesn't really matter anymore.' I stop him. 'Turns out you were right. He was everything you said he was, and worse.'

He looks at his hands thoughtfully and for once doesn't say 'I told you so'.

'I'm sorry, anyway. I really am. And I'm sorry that you're here, I should have helped you sooner.' It reminds me of the way my Mum spoke earlier. Everyone seems to be sorry. 'But I hope...' He doesn't finish and there's this potent silence where neither of us knows who should speak first. I decide to save him the trouble.

'I'm okay in here. I'll be fine.' I say, although I don't know if it's true.

Then Deano looks up at me with a fond smile on his lips that makes me want to hug him and burst into tears at the same time.

'I know you will.'

We aren't the same. This intense sadness lays heavy on my chest as I realise there's no going back. Maybe we can move on from this, it just won't be together. Some things you just have to do alone. He sighs and nods to himself then stands up to leave.

'Oh, I almost forgot,' He picks up the plastic bag and pushes it across the bed towards me. 'I managed to get this from the flat. I thought you should have it.'

I look down but can't make out the object inside. Before I can ask what it is he reaches down and catches me in a sort of half hug, half pat on the back.

'Look after yourself, Scarlet.' He was never one for overt physical affection.

Then he disappears out the door, and I know it's probably the last time we'll see each other. At least in this lifetime.

Watching Deano go leaves a new hole in my chest that will need to heal. I look at the empty space on the bed and try to tell myself it's for the best. But your heart never feels the way your head tells it to. Really it's just another loss, another abandonment, another reason to want to give up.

I sit like this for what seems like an age, paralyzed and too scared to move. Leaving this moment in the past means accepting something. I'm not quite sure what yet, but I don't know if I'm ready. Then I remember I was never one to be afraid of taking risks, so I grab the bag and pull out something grey, hard. Cold. Lauryn's camcorder. And suddenly her energy is here, as soon as my fingertips touch the smooth metal surface it's like some of her is in the room. She'd wanted to video our adventures, to document our memories. The fact that she will never see them crushes my heart into a million pieces. I don't know how long I sit like this, but soon my legs start to get pins and needles. Something urges me to switch it on, get it over with, and my thumb hovers dangerously over the power button like it's a bomb. For a second I almost change my mind and go to put the camera back in the bag, but hesitate.

Fuck it.

I click the button and the device lights up. Before I change my mind I open the screen and firmly press 'Play'. And there we are. I'm straight back to the flat and it's three months ago. Our chattering and laughing as we rack up lines. Me holding my hand up to the camera and telling Lauryn off for filming me without make-up. How can something feel so familiar yet completely foreign at the same time? We seem innocent somehow. How ironic, I think, as I watch Deano snorting and passing the DVD case to me, two neat lines prepared on the cover. It always felt so normal to us. The tape cuts to Enya's house and once more we're drinking, sniffing, laughing. It's not how I remember, but I can't explain why. It makes me uncomfortable, like some of the magic has been sucked out. And all that's left are my memories, fragmented and misplaced, viewed with new eyes that cannot marry the present with the past.

And then he's there. Jamie introduces himself to us and I'm still relieved to see my face doesn't reveal the increase in my heart rate. His hand is in mine, glasses clink, music flows from the laptop, and then we're lying on the living room floor. A heap of beautiful chaos. My heart stings each time his eyes flash towards the camera, and then Lauryn's delicate voice reverberates in my ears and it's almost too much bare. I feel the faint flutter of butterflies re-emerge in my stomach as I watch Jamie. But now they become clouded by an anger, a roaring fury that makes me want to burst.

It's all characters in a movie, scene by scene, saturated by editing and tainted by hindsight. With every gulp of beer, every popped pill and snorted line, all I feel is emptiness. I frown in confusion, watching us dance relentlessly at the rave, sitting on the dirty kitchen floor of the never-ending house party, and then it hits me.

I can't go back.

I'm tired, the kind of tired that lingers heavily round you and can be seen in your eyes. And not just that, it seems so utterly fruitless to pursue something that will never be new again. Because that's all we were doing, chasing the dream. The self-destructive part of me longs for the thrill, the drama, the recklessness. But another part now wonders if it's worth the risk, the loss, and the loneliness when the music stops and the party's over. All that remains is a grubbiness and an urge to wipe my skin clean. For the first time, I crave normality. Stability. And more than anything else, I want it to be enough. I thought it would be painful to see all our happy memories, but it's confused me all the more. The scenes playing out on the screen move to the garden rave and our babbled conversations while tripping. Lauryn had focused in on the crackling fire, and I heard Deano and I talking intensely to Oliver. The vivid colours were now bleak and ordinary, but there was a magic still alive. The camera scanned over the faces around the circle and once again I felt that palpable energy of pure connection. For a second I wonder if I'm dead, or drowning, and just witnessing my life flash before my eyes. I can't grasp it, but I want the magic back.

It suddenly becomes clear that I veered way off course somehow. I could blame a thousand things but the fact remains, I misused what was good and precious in our weird, inner world. Every thing I learned during that trip...the power of consciousness, the inescapable unity between all beings, the ever-evolving cycle of matter...has become irrelevant because I've failed to realise it outside a drug infested environment. Those truths were real, they're still real. But snorting coke like it was going out of fashion, depending on any substance to see you through the day at the cost of relationships, careers, and even lives...that was so far from what we'd realised that day. I'd just been so blind to it.

I ruined myself and those around me. And I think, I hope, I'm done now. But I'm scared. Because I don't know what happens after this, just that it's not going to be easy.

I snap the screen shut and shove the camera under the bed. It's out of sight, but a dirty, murky feeling sticks to me like a virus. I can't understand how so much of what has happened can be boiled down to a bunch of characters getting wasted, lingering on the edge of existence, stagnant and pointless. I bury my face in the pillow in the hopes it will slow down my racing mind. And now Jamie's face, his twinkling blue eyes and that cheeky smile, invade my thoughts. For about a week when I came in I went on autopilot, numb, interspersed with hysterical outbursts that made the staff call me 'difficult' like I was a troublesome toddler. But now reality is really starting to set in. When the pressure in my chest from missing Lauryn isn't all I can think about, it's him. There's been no contact. No messages, no calls, no attempt to undo the hideous mess he's helped create. I hate that I'm still inexplicably attached to him, despite everything, and how I'm now just one of his stories he'll tell when he's drunk and showing off.

Tears have been silently streaming down cheeks and I wipe my nose with my sleeve. I have a vague thought that I'm used to stuff going up my nose, not out. Everything's upside down. I'm not crying because he's gone. It's because he was never there in the first place. That person is a ghost now, and I don't know how I'll ever trust another human being again. I start to think that what I need right now is a line or two of coke, that's all. Then I'll be in a much better position to deal with the grief. I find my purse in the drawer beside my bed and open the secret zipped part inside where I used to keep my coke, meph, pills, or whatever treat I'd hidden there, and sniffed it deeply. The faint stench of chemicals felt good. So good. But that was another relationship that had gone desperately wrong. Cocaine was my best friend, my one constant. Nothing and no one ever made me feel as secure and as special. Even Jamie didn't quite reach that mark. He was flighty and unpredictable, and when I was with him I was balancing on a surfboard, exhilarated by the fury of the waves but constantly losing my footing. Coke wrapped me up safe in its arms whenever I needed it, but it had been silently dragging me in to a pit I now have to find my own way out of. Like everything else, it wasn't what it seemed.

The only thing that lures me out of bed other than mandatory groups and meal times is the urge for a smoke. Begrudgingly, I crawl into my dressing gown, the purple fluffy one that Mum brought in, and head down the hallway. I have to go through the main sitting room to reach the small smoking area outside. I keep my eyes fixed to the floor. A brief lapse in concentration could open the door to conversation and I absolutely do not need that right now. As I shuffle across the floor like a beetle, the horse-racing commentator drones incessantly on the TV. But I'm glad to find the box-sized smoking area empty and quickly claim a space on the old wooden bench. As I light up and inhale deeply, nicotine spreads soothingly through my veins. Some mild relief.

I jump irritably at the piercing squeak of the door opening and when I look up I see a large man of about sixty ambling over to me. Fantastic, I think. The bench creaks as he eases himself onto the seat beside me and starts puffing enthusiastically on a Marlborough.

'Lovely day,' he observes. This is exactly what I wanted to avoid. Human interaction. Or worst of all, idle chit chat.

'Is it?'

He must hear the agitation in my voice but it doesn't put him off.

'We'll be seeing the conkers soon.' He leans over, his giant belly sagging between his knees, and carefully picks up one of the golden leaves littered around his feet. Oh, crikey, 'Beautiful. Autumn is a very special time of year.'

'Really.' I feel a twinge of guilt when I see how content he is at the sight of this damned leaf. He seems okay in fairness, I just can't share his enthusiasm.

'Aye. A time for restoration, shedding old burdens. Maturing, as such. Just like these old oaks do.' He nods to the branches hovering over the fence, 'And look what can come of it.'

He twirls the thing between his fingers and smiles. Its bright hue glints as it catches the sunlight and I'm instantly brought back to the garden rave. I remember the sensation of the psilocybin shooting up my nose and looking in awe at the beauty of the daisies. I smile as I envisage Lauryn and I laughing like fools at the sky, how it sparkled, and how it was like seeing it for the very first time.

'It's nice to see a smile round here.'

His voice blasts me straight back to the present.

'I've seen you around the place. I'm Oscar.' The large man reaches out his chunky hand. I hesitate before taking it in mine.

'Scarlet.'

'Like the colour. Wonderful,' his eyes are honest and kind,

framed by laughter lines, and his voice is gentle and safe. 'People don't tend to come out here much. But it's important to notice these things and to appreciate it all. Get out of your own head for a while. Don't you think?'

I nod in vague agreement. My eyes drift over to the row of plant pots lined up against the brick wall to our left. The petals have mostly fallen into the soil and only a few bare twigs remain. I try to muster some emotion, any kind of feeling for my surroundings, but it's like all the air has been sucked out of me. And, infuriatingly, I find myself wondering how much better things would be if I were high right now.

'I wish I could be as positive.' I mumble out loud.

Oscar lights another cigarette and the smoke drifts and spirals up over the wall.

'Who says you can't?'

I shrug and kick the leaves around my feet.

'We make our own happiness. No one's going to save us, girl, no one and nothing. Because you're the creator, there's no such thing as fate. You're creating, all the time. And if you mess up, start over. That's the beauty of it.'

He stands up with a huge exhale of breath. I watch him carefully as he walks slowly to the door and wonder if he's a little mad.

'What are you in here for?' I blurt it out before I realise how rude it sounds.

He pauses, his hand on the handle, and turns to me with a smile.

'Drink. We all have our demons, Scarlet. Some of us are just trying to fill a hole, but we've usually made that hole ourselves. Let's hope one day we can go back to a simpler time.' He smiles but his eyes suddenly seem far away, 'Now, get yourself out of here, girl, and don't come back. There's a big world out there waiting for you.'

With that he shuffles inside. I think for a while about what he's said. My head is still too muddied to take much in, and I chain-smoke the rest of the pack. A little brown speckled bird hops around my feet, pecking at the cracks in the concrete. I cough loudly twice but he doesn't flinch. Fearless little thing, I think to myself in amusement and I realise it's been weeks since I've laughed. It's not much but it's something. And that kind of hope is what I desperately need right no.

Chapter 14

'Tell me about Jamie.' Dr Shirley says.

My back and shoulders stiffen and I start chewing my lip.

'There's nothing to tell.'

'Are you grieving for the loss of that relationship?'

'I don't really want to talk about it.' I shift in my seat and peer around the room until I find a picture frame to focus on.

'You've experienced a lot of losses in a short space of time. It's normal to feel confused, angry, or any other strong emotion.

There are no rules when it comes to grief.'

There's silence for a moment, just the faint tick of the miniature clock on Dr. Shirley's desk.

'Sometimes I'm not sure if any of it was real,' I say quietly, 'I meant nothing to him in the end. He tossed me away like old rubbish.'

'Why do you think that is?'

'I don't know, you tell me.'

'You played a role in his life. Sometimes that role isn't always what we think it is, or want it to be. But he served a purpose for you at one time, and you did to him.'

I shake my head and play with my hands.

'So he used me. If any of it meant anything to him he'd still be around.' I say bluntly.

'Not necessarily,' she leans back and chews the top of her pen again, 'Maybe, for whatever reason, it stopped serving you. And him.'

'So it wasn't meant to be, basically. I wasn't good enough for him. I know I should get over it bla bla...'

'It will stop hurting you like it is now once you stop interpreting it as a personal attack on who you are. In fact, it says little about you at all, other than that you were two people who shared an experience that you can ultimately learn and grow from. There will come a point in time where you will choose to give your time and love to someone who appreciates it. Holding on to that pain over someone who will never be who you want them to be is not only nonsensical, it's stopping you from helping yourself get better. You need to give yourself compassion. Haven't you given him enough of your time already?'

I try and see past all of her therapist-talk for a moment. Maybe, in a way, she's right.

'When will it stop hurting?' I ask.

'When you're ready to let it go.' she smiles sweetly.

'It's impossible to see a way out most of the time. I feel like I've lost everything.'

The words hang in the air uncomfortably.

'You say you've lost everything. Don't you think that, in that case, you have everything to gain?' she pauses, 'You see, it's often not our situation that makes us unhappy, but our perception of it.'

'So it's my fault I feel this way?'

'No, it's not your fault. But you do have the ability to change it. It's just a matter of learning the right tools to do so.'

'You make it sound so easy.'

'It's not easy. But I think we both know that carrying on the way things are is not an option anymore. Do you agree?' I stare at the floor in silence. 'Chasing that first high is futile, Scarlet,' she leans forward and says quietly, 'Change is inevitable, what goes up must come down. It's the nature of the world we live in. You're afraid to let go of these behaviours because you don't know how to be without them. I'm here to help you make that transition, and I think you'll find that things aren't as awful as they seem right now. And do you know what will get you there? That drive, the one that sustained your old lifestyle. The impulse to change, to grow, can be used to heal. You've just been using it in the wrong ways.'

'He used me.'

'Think about what it means to be a user. To take something off someone for your own gain.' I'm not really sure what she means but I nod. 'You can learn to not put your happiness in anyone or anything else's hands. Choosing to stop hurting yourself, choosing to take responsibility.'

When I get back to my room a staff member knocks on the door. He's a tall lanky guy with thick-rimmed glasses.

'The recovery group is on down the hall.' he says as if he's announcing a funeral,

'Oh, okay.'

I know I should probably go as it's part of my care plan. It looks good if you go to all the groups and mingle with the other 'addicts'. I just don't like the idea of it. It still feels as if I'm not like them. It's not that I'm afraid to be, or think I'm better. But there's a grave sense of defeatism in admitting yourself as an addict, it's like saying you're helpless. It removes control. The guy hovers in the doorway, looking at me expectantly.

'I might have to give it a miss,' I say, 'I've got a bit of homework from Dr. Shirley.'

It's partially true. There's something I need to do. It's too hard to explain to anyone else, but I have some crap to offload. He nods and disappears, so I grab a pen off the bedside locker and a few scraps of paper from the drawer. My hand clutches the biro, poised at the top of the page, and all at once the words begin to flow.

Jamie,

I suppose I should start by telling you what a massive twat you are, and that you probably don't deserve another moment of my time. I don't really know why I'm writing this. I could tell you how angry, humiliated and heartbroken I still am after everything you did. I could tell you how it feels to be betrayed and abandoned by someone you would have done anything for. But all I can think is what a waste it all seems, to feel like you had everything and then to lose it. Why did we have to meet only for this to happen?

It hurts so much sometimes I can barely stand it sometimes. The image of your face the first day we met haunts me during the night, and I think about how naive I was to what was to come. You appeared so suddenly, and it was like I'd been lost until that moment. I barely recognise my old self, and I'm not really sure who I am anymore. But that's how I remember you. Not distant or cowardly or with arrogance in your eyes, but boyish and filled with playfulness and passion. The man who now pretends I never existed is not the one who gently stroked my face as I slept, or the one who slow-danced with me in the bathroom to nothing but the sound of our laughter. I don't know this person who so easily forgets the past, puts on this mask and pretends that nothing ever made him look at himself, or that he shared his fear with another human being. You see, you've forgotten because you don't want to remember how utterly painful it was to let another know you were lost. But you also forget that there is no greater happiness than sharing that with someone who was just as lost as you were. I don't want anything from you other than for you to, one day, remember that. Then it won't all have been for nothing.

Love

Scarlet x

I read it about six times, but I know I'll never be fully satisfied. Maybe I'll send it to him, I'm not sure. I realise what I've written is true. I don't want anything from him, it's way past that stage now. I'm just not sure where that leaves me. But it's dinner time and I have to help set the tables, so I fold the letter carefully and put it in the back pocket of my jeans.

Oscar is waiting eagerly for tea in the dining room. He winks at me as I prepare the cutlery and I manage a smile back. It's chicken pie and chips, proper stodgy food, and I'm surprised to feel a pang of hunger as the thick smell reaches my nose. The rest of the residents trickle into the room, chairs scrape and the low hum of chatter begins to fill the silence. I manage to get a brief look at some of them but I don't want to mingle too much. I don't plan on coming back, so there's no use forging friendships in this place. There's a girl around my age who is so thin her cheekbones jut out and her fingers look like they're about to snap as she picks at bits of chicken. Opposite her is a young man who has no distinguishing features other than a large scorpion tattoo on his neck. Then there's a few middle-aged men and women conversing loudly about the NA group and how well Peter has progressed this week, whoever the hell Peter is. And of course there's Oscar, ploughing through his pie like a man on a mission. He chomps loudly and bits of sauce stick around his mouth. It's gross, but he looks content in a funny sort of way.

I manage to finish the chips and most of the pie, which is quite an achievement given my recent hunger strike. There's not much to do in the evenings, it gets kind of quiet. All the food has made me tired so I scrape my leftovers into the bin and head to my room. Just as I round the corner I see the lanky staff member talking to someone with his back to me.

'It's the residents' tea time so you're not really supposed to visit until after. But...oh, there she is.'

They both look round at me and my heart stops.

'Hi.' Jamie says.

Suddenly the chicken pie isn't sitting well in my stomach and I want to heave. I blink at him in silence, my mouth opening and closing like a moronic fish. My hair is a mess, my make-up not done, I think. My mind starts to race and with the grace of a rusty robot I lead him to my room. He hovers momentarily before sitting in the chair as I perch awkwardly on the edge of the bed. I fiddle with the cheap ring on my index finger that I picked up ages ago in a charity shop, and rub at the blue stain it's left behind. There's this awful stillness for a minute and I can feel his eyes on me. Finally, his voice breaks the silence and with it all those memories come flooding back.

'How are -'

'Why are you here?' It comes out colder than I've ever heard myself sound. Jamie is shocked at my tone and when I look up his face is strained, his eyes flickering nervously. A far cry from the effortlessly confident man that breezed into my living room just a few months before

'I just...I wanted to see how you were.' he says. His voice is warm and quiet now, and I know he's trying to draw me in. Suddenly I'm getting angry and it rapidly replaces my embarrassment. How dare he come here now, after everything, and think he can slot back into the place he so carelessly abandoned? To see how I am. Well, I'll tell you how I am. I'm furious. I've been lost and tired and scared. And it's so easy for you to come back after this violent storm has passed and ask me that...

'I'm fine.' I say instead.

I can tell by his face that he doesn't believe me, but I won't give in and spill my guts to him. I've given him enough already.

'I'm sorry, Scarlet,' he looks at me and I almost lose myself again, 'I didn't mean to hurt you.'

There's dark circles under his eyes and a shadow on his jaw where he hasn't shaved. I can only assume he's been continuing the party in my absence. But I don't envy him. I'm surprised to see just someone immature and foolish. I'm not embarrassed to be here. If anything, he should be the one who is embarrassed. Suddenly, I remember what Dr Shirley said about using and it occurred to me that I didn't love him. Love wasn't supposed to fill you with hatred and pain and desperation. He was just another addiction. And in that sense, I'd used him too.

My anger begins to diffuse the longer we sit there. He's like a warped reflection of myself, and maybe that's what had always drawn me in. That's all he is, I think to myself, a lost boy like so many others. A smile extends from the corner of my mouth as I realise a part of his grip over me has somewhat loosened.

'What are you smiling for?' he asks.

I shake my head slowly.

'Nothing,' I say finally, 'Look, I don't hate you.'

'Good,' he sighs.

'I won't forget, but I forgive you.'

I'm silently proud of myself for not falling apart. Maybe I'm growing up. My heart might always jump a little at the sound of his name, or maybe that fades in time. But all this time alone, just with myself, has sort of taught me that I can actually handle things pretty well. I think about asking him why. Just like a drug, once I start to feel in control the temptation to go back over old ground seems harmless. But I hold it in. I know I have to or I'll be right back where I started.

'I don't know what happened,' he shakes his head as if he's read my mind, 'I just have a bad habit of messing things up. But you didn't deserve it,' he pauses and peers out the window across from the bed. Crisp autumn leaves have flourished on the branches that scratch the glass pane. The sound irritated me at first, but I'm used to it now.

'I better go, I've got work,' he says, 'But maybe I can call up again tomorrow?'

He gets up and zips his jacket right up to his chin.

'I'm going to visit Lauryn's grave tomorrow.'

'Oh, ok. What about the weekend?'

'Well I've got my last therapy session and...'

I don't need to finish. He nods slowly and I think I see a faint sadness in his eyes. Regret? Maybe. Or perhaps he's just trying to ease his own conscience by coming here. I'll probably never know.

But I do know I've done something important when I let him walk away. Just as the door creaks to a close behind him, I remember the letter in my pocket. For a moment I wonder if I should give it to him. I hold it firmly in my hand. Then, without thinking twice, I walk quickly to the door. The scrunched up ball of paper barely makes a sound as it hits the bottom of the plastic bin. I won't lie, it hurts like hell all over again. But I feel stronger. That's got to count for something.

Chapter 15

Dear Lauryn,

I'm standing at your grave and I don't know if it will ever really sink in. A staff member called Susan is waiting for me in the car park, it's kind of like being a convict out on day release. But funnily enough I feel more free than I have in a long time. She said to take as long as I wanted so I want to make the most of it. God, you'd be laughing if you were here. In the rehab, they make us do things like trust exercises where you fall back and someone catches you, and then there's the arts and crafts groups. Proper cringe.

Part of me wants to draw some kind of a line under this whole saga, but it doesn't really work that way. You're gone and I will never stop missing you. You were so many things to so many people. That doesn't just disappear, does it? Sometimes it hurts so much I can hardly breathe. I hate myself for the times I didn't tell you what you meant to me, for the time I drew on your face while you were asleep and posted the photos on Facebook. You didn't even get angry, you just laughed it off. But that was just who you were, kind, loving, never a bad word leaving your mouth. The world shouldn't have to be without that.

I wonder what will become of all of us, now we've realised we're not invincible. Sometimes I slip into this black, empty state where it seems like the whole world is caving in around me, that we're going to consume ourselves into nothing despite the warnings, just like Deano said. I try and stay positive but it should never have come to this. What I'm learning, though, is that the bad stuff is always going to come around. You can't run from it. The yin and the yang, the ups and the downs. We just have to trust that we can survive the ride. I'm just scared, Lauryn. I wish more than anything that you were here to do it with me. I feel as though I'm about to embark on something alien and unpredictable, I just hope I have what it takes to see it through and make you proud.

All I really know is you were my best friend, and I let you down. You were too frail for our crazy little world and didn't deserve to be so horribly taken from it. Sometimes people come into your life that bless you simply with their presence. Their purity, their goodness, reaches everything they touch. You were an angel who brought me nothing but happiness and friendship, and your memory is the only thing that gives me hope. I cling to the belief that you have now gone back to where you belong, a place where there is no pain, untainted and peaceful. Sometimes I think the world has lost a lot of that innocence. Maybe nothing is pure anymore. There's too much anger, too much hurt, and too much fear. The reality we created was beautiful, but it also killed you. You blessed me with your friendship during your time here and I cannot thank you enough for that.

I wish I could make promises and tell you this wasn't all for nothing. But the truth is, Lauryn, I don't know. I don't know if everything's going to be alright, I don't think anyone really knows. I guess it's all about being ok with that and taking each day as it comes. The one thing I do know is I'm tired of running. I want to be better, to survive and to grow. You leaving has roused that instinct in me, and I can promise you I will fight till the very end to save myself.

But it wasn't all make believe, was it? Not in those moments. No matter what anyone says, they will never truly know the magic we made, the things we saw together. Every good thing comes to an end, though, that's what makes them so special. I have this idea that maybe you'll grow back as a daisy and I'll think of you every day of summer when they're sprawled across the lawn. So don't forget to look out for me, Lolly. Because one day we'll all be together, and everything will be beautiful again.

Love forever and always,

Scarlet x

About The Author

Abby Williams was born in England in 1990 and has been living in Belfast since the age of fifteen.

She has always been passionate about writing and studied English and International Development at the University of Ulster.

Her studies were interrupted when she suffered from a breakdown and was subsequently diagnosed with severe Obsessive Compulsive Disorder and depression.

For Abby writing is cathartic, she is currently writing two fiction novels and one non-fiction book